The Forest Speaks: Book 2 Through the Eyes of the Dragon

By

Diomira Rose D'Agostino

Diomira Rose D'Agostino
Visit my website at www.DiomiraRose.com

Printed in the United States of America
First Printing: February 2016
Published by Faery Light, LLC

ISBN: 978-1-62747-198-5
Ebook ISBN: 978-1-62747-199-2

Table of Contents

Author's Note

The Forest Speaks series deals significantly with the cycles of time upon the Earth, including the zodiacal Wheel Of The Ages as well as the Precession of the Equinoxes. The first book worked with these quite easily because there were only two such periods: nearly present day – the year 2004 – and 13,000 years ago, which was identified as 11,000 BCE.

This second book will deal with a few more time periods and the timeline for both the past and present is quite expansive. While there had been many Great Gatherings, the last Great Gathering (GG) referred to at the end of the first book was a significant event and occurred around 13,000 years ago, or about 11,000 BCE. For the sake of simplicity I will use this particular event as a time marker to better clarify to readers the time period in which the story is taking place.

In order to more easily identify the time periods through which this story moves, I have streamlined the following system:

Any time period dealing with the past will relate to the last Great Gathering, which will be abbreviated as GG. For example:

- 11,000 BCE (16 years before GG)
- 26,000 years ago (13,000 years before GG)

The more recent time periods will continue to be referred to with the corresponding year. For example:

- 2004
- 1986

Glossary
Characters and Groups

<u>Groups:</u>

Moon Clan: Community of humans that have existed for thousands of years, dedicated to protecting the ancient Faery Wisdom Teachings.

Keepers: Group of highly trained initiates within the Moon Clan who have not only dedicated themselves to the ancient Wisdom Teachings but also to the Tree Mysteries.

High Faeries: The highest expression of Faery Consciousness within the Faery Kingdom; the most highly evolved faeries who assist the Earth in her evolution.

Council of Five: High council made up of five elders of the High Faeries. Four of the elders represent their respective clans of Earth, Air, Fire and Water. The fifth is always the Record Keeper.

Air Clan: Faery clan working with the element of air. The Air Clan elder is Vayu.

Water Clan: Faery clan working with the element of water. The Water Clan elder is Seamone.

Earth Clan: Faery clan working with the element of earth. The Earth Clan elder is Aolana.

Fire Clan: Faery clan working with the element of fire. The Fire Clan elder is Leori.

Dragon Clan: Read to discover....

Characters in 11,000 BCE:

Taivyn Green: Teenage boy around 16 years old who the faeries brought to the Moon Clan as a baby. Has been raised by Moon Clan ever since.

Ra-Ma'at: Keeper of the Moon Clan who studied the Solar Mysteries. He is the twin brother of Lunaya and is 111 years old. His nickname is Sonny.

Lunaya: High Keeper of the Moon Clan, she is the twin sister of Ra-Ma'at, and also 111 years old.

Astriel: Keeper of the Moon Clan, her work is with animals.

Lir: Keeper of the Moon Clan, his work is concentrated on being a Watcher, one who watches the energy fluctuations of the Earth.

Telzar: Keeper of the Moon Clan who is mysterious in his nature. He lived with Rock Trolls for a while.

Korin: Keeper of the Moon Clan who stays at the community training the younger children and teens in the Path of the Keeper.

Jonah: An elder within the Moon Clan; he is also a master healer.

Lomi: Moon Clan member.

Amelda: Old woman in the *Forest*. Read to discover more….

Characters who exist outside of Time:

Elysinia: High Faery elder and member of the Council of Five. She is the Record Keeper. She is the mother of Rose and Elrin.

Vayu: High Faery elder and member of the Council of Five. He is the elder of the Air Clan. He is the husband of Vayanna.

Vayanna: High Faery of the Air Clan; she is also the beloved wife of Vayu.

Leori: High Faery elder and member of the Council of Five. He is the elder of the Fire Clan. He is the husband of Leona.

Leona: High Faery of the Fire Clan; she is also the beloved wife of Leori.

Seamone: High Faery elder and member of the Council of Five. She is the elder of the Water Clan.

Aolana: High Faery elder and member of the Council of Five. She is the elder of the Earth Clan.

Rose: High Faery and daughter to Elysinia. She is the past incarnation of Jedda.

Rael: High Faery Page who assists Elysinia in her work with the crystals.

Elrin: High Faery; he aspires to sit on the Council of Five. He is the son of Elysinia.

Guinevere: High Faery; friend to Rose; she intends to become human; daughter of Leori and Leona.

Wilma: High Faery of the Air Clan; she is the leader of the Tribe of the North Winds.

Jory: Gnome who has several children and lives in a tree.

Gorlin: Gnome King

Wallen: Gnome

Archer Spider: A spider who lives in the Forest; friend to Jory and lives in same tree enclosure.

Yuri: A raven known as The Messenger, or *one who walks between the worlds*; an intermediary who walks through time. Works with Lunaya often. Also in service to the High Faeries.

Characters in Present (2005)

Jedda Delaney: Teenage girl of about sixteen. Lives in present-day Maine, but has a connection with the past and the *Forest*. She is Rose reincarnated, so she was once Faery. Training to be the next Keeper.

Mr. Ramen: Jedda's English teacher. The reincarnation of Ra-Ma'at.

Lou Silverton: Jedda's previous history teacher, Lou is the current Keeper of the Moon Clan. The reincarnation of Lunaya.

Artemis: A Keeper's Cat; he is currently Jedda's cat. He previously belonged to the Grandmother.

Isis: A Keeper's Cat; she is currently the cat of Lou.

Diane Delaney: Jedda's mother.

Jake Delaney: Jedda's younger brother.

Jim Delaney: Jedda's father.

Malin: Read to discover more…

Vyncent: Belongs to Malin's group of boys. Read to discover more…

Gus: Belongs to Malin's group of boys. Read to discover more….

The Grandmother: Also known as Elda. The eldest Keeper and member of the Moon Clan, however she has relinquished the responsibility as now there is only one Keeper at a time. She is also Lou's aunt.

Katerina: Member of the Moon Clan; wife to Joe.

Joe: Member of the Moon Clan; husband to Katerina.

Prologue

*"Our outstanding contribution to the
planet is our developed capacity to love;
we can go deeply into the Heart of Love."*

– Dorothy Maclean, *To Hear the Angels Sing*

The Forest – 11,000 BCE (6 months after GG)

S he would not look back again. From this point on
there was only forward. She stepped beyond the
two standing columns and entered the bridge. She took
several more steps, and then Rose was gone.

Those standing in wait were so still they almost
held their breath. For three days they would work and
wait for Rose to appear on the other end. Three days.
The Frog and the Mushroom would commune for this
length of time. It was a song; it was a dance; it was a
meeting of power.

With her soft, delicate hands, Elysinia held tightly
the crystal. It took the efforts of many to focus this raw
power. And focus it they had for the good of the whole,
thus the Rainbow Bridge was created.

No one saw the Dark One who lurked in the
shadows, watching for the time when he might unfurl
his plan. And so the keen observer waited – until just
the right moment to strike....

Then the ground shook. Thunder sounded as if ripping the atoms within the atmosphere to shreds. A reddish-pink lightning never before seen struck and shattered the sky. Chaos. Animals scrambled and dashed for cover. Screams were heard. Confusion. No one knew what was happening except the Mother Earth who wept. And then everything went black.

Only darkness remained. For everyone.

Chapter 1
Silver Scale

"Humanity awakens slowly. Matter-blinded through the centuries, few men as yet perceive the Mind within the substance, the Life within the form."

- Geoffrey Hodson, *The Kingdom of the Gods*

The Forest – 11,000 BCE (16 years before GG)

"There is a darkness that hovers around mankind. Soon it will spread and affect even those of the Moon Clan. Have you not all seen the stories within the tree rings? We must decide at which point we choose to disengage and retreat into the Mists, and leave the humans to themselves." The flames around his form lurched as Leori voiced his opinion. Golden threads of fiery light twisted and wound their way through his hair that was more like a mane. This faery elder had seen enough.

"Leori, do we really do them a service by deserting them at this crucial time within the Ages?" Seamone wondered. A watery milieu of waveforms moved around her body. Indigo and blue hues gave way to sea-foam green rays. She waved her hands through these colors sporadically, helping the emotions to flow and not settle.

The slamming of Leori's staff shook the ground, and was followed by a curt retort: "Do we not do them a great disservice by forcing their hand when there exists so little willingness? Darkness has all but consumed their hearts and clouded their minds!"

A wind blew from everywhere and nowhere. Vayu was deeply conflicted by the issue. He knew the council must come to some form of agreement. Their greatest strength was in unity. Logic and reason were the gifts of this faery elder of the Air Clan. He moved for clarification, "Is it not now, more than ever, so important that we try to strengthen our alliance? If we continue to stand together perhaps all will not be lost during the Age of Sleep...."

Elysinia spoke now, her tone loving but firm, "Leori is correct in his conjecture that no good ever comes by forcing one's will upon another, even if the cause be noble. However there are still those who wish to work side by side. Until the day comes when this is not so, I believe we must continue to work together with the humans."

Visible through the oculus was the starlit sky. The opening rested in the high earthen ceiling above, and was the only connection to the surface in this dome-like subterranean cave. Elysinia's golden hair gleamed in the starlight. The glow of her skin shone through her silken garment of silver and violet. She turned to Vayu, acknowledging that she had heard his concerns as well.

"It is also right to understand the importance of our partnership with the humans. Do not forget that our destiny is deeply intertwined with theirs. Although we have grown along different paths we are still connected through our Earthly home, as well as...." Before Elysinia could finish her point, Rael appeared from the tunnels.

A faery page who was Elysinia's right hand in every way, Rael approached respectfully: "Elysinia, forgive my intrusion, but you must come to the East Mound Entrance at once. There is something you are going to want to see."

Elysinia looked at the others, who nodded their understanding. They were a long way away from mutual agreement, but with more time perhaps....

"We shall adjourn the meeting for now. Let us resume the discussion at the first Quarter Moon."

Elysinia excused herself from the room that held the large Round Table. Gliding swiftly down the long corridor that led to the outskirts of the kingdom, she knew full well that Rael would not have considered interrupting if something weren't of the utmost importance.

Tall and sparkling was this being, just like all of the Faery Ones. His eyes, a bluish grey with specks of gold, were deeply hypnotic but often cool and distant. Royal blue attire always graced his form, and his demeanor was noble and true. Rael had been working with

Elysinia for over 3,000 years. The crystals held him in fascination, and nothing brought him greater joy.

The corridor came to an end, offering a myriad of directions in which to proceed. Twists and turns were prevalent and one who did not know these underground tunnels well would consider themselves to be forever lost within a maze of a thousand choices. The tunnels connected to the innermost rooms and were necessary to guard the most precious and sacred treasures, not the least of which were the crystals, which lay within the walls of the Crystal Library.

They did not tarry; Rael and Elysinia took no thought as they made their way around the curling passageways, traveling farther out of the Earth toward the surface.

Rael offered no information. Either he had none to give, or he thought to allow the situation to speak for itself, Elysinia did not know. As they approached the East Mound Entrance, a tiny shriek filled the air. Elysinia's attention was suddenly drawn to a shadowy and pallid form. Held and sheltered within the folds of a mysterious hooded woman's long dark cape, a tiny infant cried out. The woman struggled to maintain her footing, and one of the four faery scouts who were standing nearby moved quickly, offering himself as a brace to steady her. Holding the baby with her one arm, the debilitated woman reached out for Elysinia with the other.

Visibly unwell, she attempted to mutter an explanation: "You are She Who Records Time, yes..." the woman managed.

"Yes, I am Elysinia. What brings you here to our borders in such dire straits?"

"You and I are more familiar than you know, although my condition makes me nearly unrecognizable to you or anyone of your kind or another. There is no time for explanation, though, for my time is not long now."

The feeble woman looked at the baby, "Please. You must help me. Help him. He is the last."

"The last…?" Elysinia was confused momentarily.

Just as the realization began to dawn the woman spoke again, "Yes, My Lady. He is the last of the Dragon Clan." As those final words fell from her lips her form began to dissolve. Dispersed as if by wind, she grew ethereal, and flickered in and out of existence.

Understanding the gravity of the situation, the faery elder uttered, "Wait! Of what House is he? How will I properly train him? I must know from which one of the four Houses he hails!"

Coming from all directions, an echo was heard on the wind as it whispered through the trees, "He was born with the Silver Scale."

Embedded in the center of the baby's tiny wrist was a tiny silver dragon scale. It gleamed in the light of the moon that hung low and full this night. *The mark of the Silver Prince*, thought Elysinia. The baby floated in midair. Then by some unseen force, he gently arrived in Elysinia's arms.

In the place where the woman had stood, a swirling silver-white mist filled the air, and something materialized there. The baby who had been crying incessantly suddenly became silent, and a tiny sound like a giggle arose from his lips. A glimpse of what appeared to be the silhouette of a silver Dragon flashed before their eyes. And just as soon as it had emerged, it was gone, as if it were never even there.

Chapter 2
Here There Be Dragons

*"The mind's limits being miraculously loosed,
they clearly and most plainly behold the whole
of the earth, together with the circuit of the
oceans and the heavens, in one single moment,
as if beneath a single ray of sun."*

-Vita Columbae I. 43

California – 1998

"There was a time long ago when dragons roamed the Earth."

Eyes rolled as the old man began his tale. Unmoved by one of the young boys' reaction, he sat dignified and tall, his long white beard trailing down the front of his green and blue dress shirt. The old man continued his tale confidently, knowing that what he was about to speak was the absolute truth.

"When the Earth was born so too were the dragons upon it. There was not a time when the Earth was and the dragons were not. They were with her from the beginning."

"Sir, we want to learn about stuff that is real." One of the boys had been brave enough to voice what most, if not all, were thinking.

No respect, absolutely none, thought the old man. He let out a sigh that said without saying that this was going to be a long day.

Why are the children of today so petulant?

He continued, unwilling to allow the youth of today to defeat him in his efforts. After all, even if he only reached one....

"Intergalactic beings that work on a planetary level to maintain balance through their movement, the dragons come to inhabit a planet at its inception and stay through to its end, or at least until the planet learns to maintain its own energy in a balanced and consistent way. Like training wheels, the dragons help us remember how to move so we don't fall down. Of course planets don't really fall down, do they? No, not quite. But they can get out of balance."

There were no more objections, as the boys had obviously conceded to the elder's authority. Having quickly learned that there was no winning this one, silence was the only response to the continued telling of the tale. The old man was a gentle soul, but determined was he in delivering the lessons he had set out to teach that day. Staying on task was particularly important to him. After all, he hadn't traveled all this way for nothing. Besides, he could feel that they were close. He had a feeling they would find the one for whom they searched very soon.

"The Age of Dragons was a glorious age for the Earth, for all of Earth's creatures lived and worked in harmony. There was no conflict, only peace, for all still perceived the One Reality and saw themselves as part of the whole of creation. To be in conflict meant to be out of sorts with oneself, and that just wouldn't do.

"Now the dragons sleep, being able to assist more effectively on the dream plane. It has been…" The old man had been interrupted before finishing his sentence.

"Does every planet have dragons?" One of the boys was particularly engaged. The boy seemed tall, but the old man knew that based on the group's average age the boy couldn't be more than ten or eleven years old. His eyes possessed an unusual eagerness that the old man rarely saw in his young students nowadays, even those whose parents were of his enlightened organization.

"My dear boy, one must focus on here and now. One must be where one is. You are just beginning to learn about the vastness and diversity of the Earth. If you get too distracted with what is outside you will never learn what is within. Now let us not get carried away with ourselves just yet. Hmm…."

Anxious to understand, the boy piped down. Like ripples in a small pond the boy's eyes shifted from grey green to emerald the more intently he focused. Oftentimes these classes would have him dreaming of playing with horses – an animal that he loved and often wished he had – but daydreaming was not for today.

Fumbling with a small metal button on his shirt, he was determined to listen to this story.

The old man continued, "It has been thousands of years since the dragons have been awake and no one really remembers who they are or what they are like. Some tell tales of them having a fierce temper, bellowing fire like it was pouring flames.

"Truth be told I've heard a very different tale that begins and ends quite a different way, and I'd like to share it with you today. If you wish me to stop here I'm sure you could go on as if nothing significant in your life has changed. However, you are forewarned that if you choose to continue I release any and all responsibility for completely altering your perception of reality and any ideas you may or may not have had about dragons. Now I cannot tell you really how or when this all begins, but I can recount to you the beginning of the end, and that is really where our story shall begin.

"Here is the story as it was told to me:

"As I mentioned, there was a time long ago when dragons were just as common as you or I, or foxes, rabbits and trees, for that matter. In fact, dragons had the upper hand and ruled. This was not because they were particularly domineering or ill-tempered, but because they were the most powerful and respected creatures on the Earth. Their wisdom far surpassed what we today would consider sheer brilliance. They were powerful, courageous and most of all noble-hearted. If you had the great honor of making a dragon's acquaintance you were truly blessed."

While the boys remained silent, the old man could tell they were dubious of what he shared – except for the one boy with the emerald eyes. He listened intently, unwilling to miss a word of the old man's story. Satisfied he had the attention of at least one of them, the old man came to the most exciting part of his story.

"Now once in a while there would come along a rare soul on a most auspicious occasion when all the stars were aligned in a particular way, on a specific day, in a particular month (the weather was a factor, too, however I am not privy to that information). On this most auspicious occasion, this rare soul would have the great opportunity to form an alliance with a dragon."

The old man closed the book and peered over at the intensely focused young boy who sat before him. With that the old man began telling a history that had more to do with the young apprentice than they both could have ever imagined.

Chapter 3
Good Morning, World!

"Two fairies it was
On a still summer day
Came forth in the woods
With the flowers to play."

– Robert Frost, *"Spoils of the Dead"*

Maine – 2005

J edda rose bright and early this Saturday morning. This had not been a typical routine of hers in the past of course, as Jedda had never been a morning person. She had never taken well to rising early on Saturday mornings – ever! She recalled the glorious era when, like every normal teenager, beauty sleep had been a regular part of her weekend schedule.

Nowadays things were a little different. For starters, she was slowly but surely coming to realize that she didn't seem to fit in with the rest of humanity. A proper comparative analysis would show that activities such as walking through tree portals and talking to plants, animals and beings that others couldn't see would constitute a far cry in hell from the norm. Then again who really was normal? Certainly not those girls who couldn't talk about anything besides fashion and nail polish! Or the boys who were so into sports they believed that all of life was one big competition! She sighed.

It wasn't that she didn't talk to anyone; she just didn't talk to anyone about all *this*. Heck, what could she say? She imagined a fairly typical conversation:

Jedda: "So how was your weekend?"

Reply: "I went to a party on Friday night and hung out at the mall all day Saturday. What about you?"

Jedda: "Oh you know, the usual. I traveled through a tree to another world and then relaxed on Sunday talking to my cat and the faeries."

Yeah right. She'd be the laughing stock of the whole school. Being the subject of other people's cruel jokes did not sit high on her bucket list. Ridicule was to be avoided at all costs. The last thing she needed was to be cast out from the few acquaintances she had, which in short meant that when it came to personal stuff, conversation was kept to a minimum. She would not discuss any of it with anyone – well, anyone except Lou Silverton.

Jedda had found Lou immensely engaging as a history teacher. History had never really been a topic of much interest to her, but something about the way Lou taught it made the subject come alive. She had Jedda captivated from day one of her sophomore year. Figures throughout history became actual people with stories and voices. Civilizations and cultures came alive through their art, literature and archeological remains. Lou would incorporate all of these elements when presenting the subject.

Then one day a question about a symbol changed everything about their relationship forever. Who could have known that the mesmerizing information Lou offered during class wasn't even the tip of the iceberg when it came to what this woman really knew? Ever since that day things had never been the same. Of course life had already gotten strange before that – with talking birds and strange dreams, the young girl had thought she was losing her mind. Jedda didn't know what she would have done if it hadn't been for Lou.

No doubt it had been a shock when Lou had privately revealed to Jedda the astonishing tale of who she really was – a Keeper of the Moon Clan. What had been much harder to process, however, was the riveting revelation that Jedda herself was somehow part of this lineage as well!

Now as she neared the end of her junior year, Jedda reflected back on it all. She couldn't believe it had actually been a full revolution around the sun since all this had first happened. Her relationship with Lou had changed significantly since then. For starters, Lou was no longer Jedda's history teacher. Jedda had graduated from her class with flying colors. As a junior, Jedda was forced to take government, which she appalled. How boring learning about due process was!

Luckily they had continued meeting on a regular basis during after-school hours. This was, of course, the only reason Jedda was so awake on this Saturday morning. History was not, however, the subject of interest when they met – at least not in the traditional sense.

Jedda knew very little about what they would be talking about today. Her curiosity having gotten the best of her, Jedda had phoned Lou this past Thursday evening to inquire about the upcoming weekend's lessons. Lou had only given her one thing to go on: dragons! Jedda recalled their conversation.

"Dragons?" Jedda was shocked. What could she mean?

"Yes, Jedda. Dragons."

"What about dragons?"

"Well, you will just have to wait and see."

Jedda loved when Lou taught using myth and symbols. Sometimes an understanding would occur way beyond what her conscious mind was computing. The way Lou taught with symbols was riveting. The symbols, when strung together, were like some ancient language that spoke to Jedda's soul. They would usually talk while walking among the trees in the woods behind Lou's house.

Evolet Woods always provided the best backdrop for this sort of teaching. Gnomes would usually trail the two of them as they made their way along the old footpath that led to the stream. Like a nature sanctuary where the doorway between the worlds was thin and easily passed through, these woods were known for the magic that lived there. Just a ways inward there was an area called Faery Glen. Its beauty was untamed and enchanted. And in its center was an ancient labyrinth.

Excited for what the day might hold, Jedda popped out of bed. In so doing, she unwittingly disturbed Artemis, and he let out a loud meow to let her know. She patted him gently on the head.

"Sorry Artemis. I didn't mean to wake you. You were really cute there all curled up. I'm just really excited. I'm going to visit Lou today. If you want to come, just let me know. You could see Isis."

Artemis meowed, stretched his long, black, furry body and laid his head back down. He shut his eyes and returned to his peaceful slumber as if nothing had happened. She wasn't sure what that meant. That was okay; he could decide when she got ready to leave.

She danced over to her special corner. Lou had been teaching her the art of meditation; to Jedda it seemed to be more of a chore than an art. Lou explained that all the answers anyone ever needed could be found by going within. Meditation helped to connect one to their own inner light. Jedda thought of it like an email to the heart and mind of the Universe. How exciting!

Plopping down on a soft green floor pillow, she prepared for takeoff. Five, four, three, two, one…blast off. Well…not quite. Jedda was still practicing. She took a few deep breaths to still her mind. Then she said a brief, but heartfelt opening prayer that connected her to the sacred space, just as Lou had taught her. She was excited, so much so in fact that she failed to calm her thoughts, or still her mind. What could be said? She was still learning. She wondered at how someone who could journey through a tree portal so easily could have such a difficult time concentrating.

She decided to give it one last shot, and started chanting sacred tones to help her focus: "Om. Om. Om." Lou had said that the sacred Om syllable led to the creation of the universe. There she went again, thinking. *Rats! Focus, Jedda. Focus!* she commanded herself. "Om Mani Padme Hum." She wasn't even studying Buddhism, but she liked the sound of the chant.

Finally she hopped up from the pillow undiscouraged. Lou said not to worry if she didn't have a profound experience every single time. The important thing was that she stuck with it. "Set the time aside and make it a habit," was Lou's gentle but firm instruction.

She went to her bookshelf and pulled out a brand new journal. She never did get that other one back from Jake; he had completely denied having any part in the disappearance of it. She knew he was lying, but she didn't care. It took a lot more than that to get her down these days. She opened the shiny covered book and made a comfy spot next to her cat on the bed.

I wonder if Artemis ever meditates, she thought to herself. She waved the idea away. He was wise enough, and she guessed he didn't need to add to his wisdom. Jedda chuckled at the thought of him meditating. Soon she had such a hilarious image conjured up of him sitting on a pillow with his paws contorted in some strange cat mudra that she nearly fell off the bed laughing. Artemis meowed, indicating she'd obviously disturbed him once again. She couldn't help it.

"Artemis, I know you are trying to sleep, but it's time for you to get up, lazy bones. Anyway, you are not going to believe this, but I just had the funniest vision of you meditating!"

Barely managing to spit out the last words, she burst into an uproar once again. Artemis was clearly not amused. He sniffed at her, got up, turned around so that his back was to her. He kneaded the blanket to recreate a spot and resettled himself.

A lot of research said that pets could take on certain qualities of their owners. She thought about her usual distaste at being woken up, and smiled. Looking over at Artemis sleeping peacefully once again, she knew he was definitely her cat. Jedda turned her attention to getting dressed and ready for the day ahead.

Chapter 4
Evolet Woods

"Though the doorways to the enchanted realms may be obscure, there are methods for seeking them out."

– Ted Andrews, *Enchantment of the Faerie Realm*

Maine – 2005

T he day turned out to be a dreary one. The sky was a sheet of gray with gloomy clouds blotting out the light of the sun. Luckily it had rained the night before, and so it seemed the worst of it was over. Jedda arrived on Lou's doorstep five minutes early. Undiscouraged by the melancholy tone of the day, she excitedly reached out to ring the doorbell. Milliseconds before her fingertip touched the cold metal button that would notify Lou of her arrival, a loud cawing pierced the otherwise somber overtone that pervaded.

Jedda looked up to see if perchance the sound originated from the raven that she had come to know and like very much. While she hadn't seen him in quite a while, a few months at least, Jedda was sure they were due for a visit soon. The raven had played such a significant role in her life over the past year.

Yuri was the raven's name and he was not from this place or time, and yet he seemed to easily "walk between the worlds," as he called it. It was Yuri who had guided her to come inside the large and majestic willow tree that adorned her front yard. That had been her first experience with tree portaling, or using a tree to slip into another realm. Since that first time, tree portaling had become second nature for the young girl.

Who needs parties or prom when you can escape the world through a tree?

Jedda brushed her long, brown hair out of her face. While it was not sunny, the daylight was easiest stared into if muted ever so slightly, and so Jedda brought her hand up over her eyes to create a bit of a shade. Nothing. She didn't glimpse any birds flying overhead let alone the raven she had hoped to see. Leaning back hoping to spot something, she lost her footing and slipped on the wet steps. Before she knew it she was tumbling to the ground. Her reflexes snapped into action, and her hands were out bracing for the fall, but none too soon. While her hands had buffered her impact, they could not prevent the crash. With a thud she landed hard on the wet cold ground, her hands and arms throbbing. More shaken than actually hurt, Jedda breathed a sigh a relief that it had not been worse.

Clumsy idiot. You can travel through a tree but you can't maintain your balance on a doorstep.

Slightly disgusted with herself, Jedda had started to pull herself up from the pavement when the door opened. It only took seconds for the situation to register.

"Jedda, honey, what happened? Are you okay?" The concerned tone in Lou's voice must have indicated Jedda looked a little worse than her initial assessment led her to believe.

"Jedda, you are bleeding."

Lou ran to Jedda's side to help her off the ground. She assisted her inside, and sat her down on the sofa in front of the fire. The caring mentor disappeared around the corner. When she reappeared she was carrying Band-Aids and an herbal ointment made from plantain leaf. Lou had a knack for herbs. Really every member of the entire Plant Kingdom was friend to her. Lou adjusted her glasses to assess the damages. Fortunately they amounted to no more than a few scrapes and cuts. Applying the cream gently to the wounded areas, Lou had Jedda patched up in no time.

"Thanks, Lou. Really, I'm fine. I just slipped. Dumb, really. I thought I saw Yuri, and that's when I fell. I was looking up. How embarrassing!"

"Nonsense. Don't be so hard on yourself. Gentleness is the key that unlocks closed doors."

"Hmmphh! You should talk." A large black and silver feline thumped down the hallway.

"Oh Isis. What do you know?" Lou teased her cat.

"Well, for starters, you could take your own advice, and be gentle with *yourself.*"

23

"Yes, well, I suppose we could all be more gentle with ourselves," Lou admitted sheepishly. Her soft honeycomb curls rustled as she got up.

"Jedda, why don't you relax here on the sofa while I make us a pot of tea. Then we can see if you are still up for our lesson."

Jedda jumped to her feet. "Of course, I am still up for our lesson. Lou, I look forward to our Saturday sessions all week. I'm not going to let a little fall stop this adventure. Come on. I am fine."

"Oh all right. I know. I just want to be sure," Lou replied as she made her way into the kitchen to start the water boiling.

"Lou, you can be sure. I am fine."

"Okay good. Because it is perfect weather for what we intend to do."

It is?

Jedda wondered if Lou was joking. The dampness from last night's rain made it seem colder than it was and the ground must have been soaked. She gazed over at the fire as it burned and crackled. Jedda didn't mind the rain, nor did she mind the cold. That was, as long as she wasn't actually wet and cold.

There was an array of floor pillows near the hearth, spread out and welcoming. Jedda got up from the sofa to make her way over to the inviting plush cushions. She crawled onto what appeared to be a small blue mound and made herself comfortable. This would help her dry off a bit before their walk in the woods.

Lou returned shortly with a steaming pot of tea that rested atop a tray among an assortment of mismatched teacups. Lou knew how Jedda enjoyed choosing her own cup. She always selected something to mirror the mood she was in. A brightly colored cup the shade of an apple was Jedda's mug of choice on this rainy day, which meant that despite the gloomy weather and the unwelcome accident, Jedda was rather upbeat and ready for an adventure. Lou smiled in regard to the girl's particularly optimistic attitude.

"So where's Artemis? Did you bring him?" Isis meowed questioningly from her spot on one of the other pillows, the one closest to the fire.

"No, I have to confess he declined emphatically." Jedda laughed, "He'd rather sleep than come over and enjoy company."

"Suits me just fine," Isis uttered, her meow like an intonation.

Jedda and Lou laughed together. Those two cats were two peas in a pod. No wonder they didn't want to share in each other's company too often. Having just one of them around was plenty to handle.

"So I thought we would begin today inside while we sipped our tea. Then, if you are up for it…," Lou stopped short because Jedda had furled her eyebrows in an expression that said she did not want to be coddled. Lou got the hint and poured some tea into their cups.

"Okay, I know you are fine. It's just my overprotective nature, I'm sure. Anyway, we shall still begin inside, and then make our way into the woods."

Jedda brightened, "Are we going to discuss dragons?" She wanted to know. Lou had indicated that would be their subject of discussion when she asked her several days ago.

To Jedda's disappointment, Lou responded, "I'm afraid not. I have decided that I would prefer one of my colleagues to deliver that teaching to you."

Drooping shoulders indicated that Jedda was dissatisfied. She had been so excited about the prospect of learning about dragons, even if it was symbolic, which oftentimes it was. She lamented in her head one last time, and then moved on.

"You have colleagues?" Quickly over the disappointment, Jedda had moved on to the next subject. Dwelling had never suited her personality and she wouldn't indulge in it today.

"Yes, and I believe he is better suited to explain the nature of…."

Jedda was so eager she didn't let Lou finish, "So what are we going to learn today?" Not characteristically rude, Jedda didn't mean to cut her teacher off. However, her enthusiasm sometimes got the better of her. When that happened she tended to talk incessantly. Lou's patience was cultivated and mature, just like her wisdom. For that reason, she smiled as she took a sip of her tea. Lou lifted her chin softly indicating that Jedda's tea was going to get cold. No one liked cold tea, especially not on a day with a chill in the air.

"The forest. Today we will learn about the forest."

Jedda's eyes grew big. Whether talking about them or to them, trees were a favorite of hers. She loved how they seemed to grow toward the stars, ever aspiring to touch the heavens. Yet they were deeply rooted in the Earth, their root system sometimes stretching forever into the depths. Walking through the forest always cultivated a sense of wonder. Jedda recalled her time she'd spent in *the Forest* – the one that lay in the other time.

As if reading her thoughts, Lou continued, "Jedda, you shared much about your journey in the other world, the other time. However, it is important to understand that the Forest you experienced is not separate from the forest behind my home."

Jedda's eyes grew even wider. She had never really thought about it until now, but perhaps she had thought of them as separate, different even.

"Come, Jedda."

The forest behind Lou's home was called Evolet Woods. An old growth forest, it contained many species of trees that one did not always find growing together anymore. Not because different trees didn't naturally grow alongside one another. On the contrary, trees enjoyed diversity, and, like a soul group, thrived when allowed to grow in this way. Unfortunately the trees, or *Standing People* as the natives liked to call them, were very rarely left to their own devices. Evolet Woods, however, was unscathed by the touch of humans.

Jedda knew the woods were special. Even without Lou, Jedda would come here in the afternoons to walk among the magical green things growing in this place. Lou's was one of the only houses on the North side of the park, and so one could easily enjoy solitude on most days. No one besides them really came to the woods anymore. *How sad*, Jedda thought. *No one takes time to listen to the trees.*

They stepped onto the ground made soft by last night's rain.

"The water wakes everything up. The life force is most palpable after a good rain."

So that's why Lou said it was perfect weather conditions.

Almost immediately Jedda could feel the soft, effervescence in the ground and air to which Lou surely was alluding. Out of the corner of her eyes, willowy wisps of light caught Jedda's attention. As soon as she turned to get a closer look, the shimmering forms vanished. Lou noticed Jedda's preoccupation with something to the left of them and smiled.

She sees the magic here. Good. Her eyes are aligning with her heart.

On other occasions Jedda had noticed the gnomes trailing them, but the wisps were less tangible. These luminous creatures weren't as easy to discern in the physical world. Then again, this wasn't exactly the physical world.

"Shall we walk some?" Lou asked, prompting Jedda to follow closely by her side as they ventured deeper into the woods. They arrived at a small stream that trickled from the Northern border and wound its way through the center of the woods. Just beyond the Northern rock-cropped border was a magical meadow known to the locals as Faery Glen. At its center lay an age-old labyrinth. Some say it had been constructed by the early settlers that had emigrated from the Old

World. Others insisted its stones were not laid by the settlers but by the natives that once walked freely and proudly upon these lands.

They tarried along the rocks and boulders, and then curved to the West. The labyrinth would be for another day. Today their place was among the trees. Jedda marveled at the giant oaks and Eastern hemlocks. There were many ash and hawthorn, too.

"Really all forests are one, Jedda. The Forest that you were in was very special. It exists somewhere between here and there."

Yes, like a dream.

That was how Jedda had remembered it. Like an ethereal paradise, the Forest to which Jedda had journeyed was otherworldly, hanging on the edges of a dream.

Lou continued, "Even though you experienced events that occurred long ago, the Forest is timeless. It serves as a bridge. Moreover it acts as a mainframe, and all the forests the world over are connected to it on some level. Even if they don't exist here any longer."

Jedda thought about the roots of trees that spread far below the ground they walked on now. Even on the physical earth, the roots connected one tree to another, and also, through the soil, connected them to the entire planet.

"Look!" Lou said. Jedda looked up through the nearly leafless tree branches. A raven was perched high up on the loftiest branch of a large oak tree. Jedda spotted the black bird just before he cawed and took flight. When he was out of view Jedda returned her gaze to eye level.

Almost to herself, Jedda asked aloud, "But why doesn't he make contact?"

"Perhaps it wasn't him?" Lou saw the disheartened look on the girl's face.

"It was him. It was definitely him." Jedda was certain it had been Yuri. Why he was keeping his distance she was not sure.

Eager to cheer her apprentice, Lou offered, "Come on, Jedda. Let's make our way back and have some lunch, shall we?"

That certainly brightened Jedda's mood. No longer downtrodden, Jedda perked considerably as they found their way back through Evolet Woods and to Lou's home.

Chapter 5

A Darkness So Deep

"The fairies are connected to the vitality of the land."

-Robert Kirk, *The Secret Commonwealth of Elves,*
Fauns and Fairies

The Forest – 11,000 BCE (Day 2 of GG)

"This darkness...have you all felt it?" Ra-Ma'at wanted to know if he was alone in his concern. Somewhat agitated, he stroked his long white beard. The Solar Keeper was apprehensive and rushed.

The Great Gathering had been in session for two full days and nights. A meeting of those who sought to support the Earth as she moved through the ages, the Great Gathering was comprised of not only the Faery Council of Five and many of the Moon Clan elders, but a plentitude of animals as well. It was well attended even by many other members of the Faery Kingdom, which spoke volumes of its significance for all walks of life upon the planet.

Rose, Elysinia's daughter, had been introduced on the first day, and with her, a possible solution to preserving the ancient Faery Wisdom Teachings. Crossing over from faery to human consciousness, Rose would endeavor to hold within her heart the memory of the ancient secrets of the Earth and Sky, the Language of the Trees, and most of all human and faery partnership. If ever the Line of Keepers should fail, there would be Rose, who would surely remember. Having said all there was to say on this, the discussion had moved to more immediate concerns.

"Perhaps it is the Turning of the Ages that you are perceiving, no?" Astriel wanted to know. Her ebony black hair was braided and wrapped in a bun, making it difficult to see that it fell so long. Small tendrils framed her perfectly heart-shaped face from which dark and piercing almond eyes stared out and gently entranced all who engaged with her. When she spoke, her powerful voice belied her particularly petite and gentle form. As one of the Moon Clan Keepers, her opinion meant a great deal. Yet her focus had always been on working with the animals, not the elements.

"I don't think so, Astriel. There is something more. Something building, growing, gaining strength. Something that lies underneath the natural feeling of change. A foreboding…." Lunaya, the Moon Clan's High Keeper, had felt it, too. The Keeper's tall form, statuesque and bold, commanded a presence that begged to be listened to. Misleading were her porcelain skin and rich golden hair, as her age was well past one hundred years.

Lir agreed, "Yes, yes. I've felt that. But when I make any attempt to attune and have a clearer look, it's like I run into a wall." While also an elder and Keeper within the Moon Clan, Lir's path led to becoming a Watcher, or one who connects with the energy of the Earth and watches for change. Lir was of mid-sized height for a man, but very strong. His honey blond hair rested perfectly on his head. A maroon cape hung around his shoulders and fell to the ground, giving him a stately appearance. His senses were shrewd and keen. Lir's inability to clearly perceive this unusual energy was an indication of its adept concealment.

"Yes, the Dark One has cloaked himself well…," Aolana mused. Her starlit skin gleamed underneath her flower-filled garment.

"The Dark One…?" Ra-Ma'at wondered aloud. By the looks on the faces of the other Moon Clan members, they were just as clueless as he. They looked questioningly at the Faery Council of Five for answers.

"Yes, we are aware that an interesting cocktail of energy has been brewing for the last couple of years. There is someone stirring things up." The flames danced and sizzled through Leori's hands and arms as he spoke. His temper was beginning to kindle. His distrust for humans revealed itself.

Elysinia had not spoken since Rose's plan had been revealed the day before. She and her daughter had envisioned it together. However, once the idea was delivered, natural motherly tendencies took her by surprise. Suddenly she had been overcome with the hard realization that her daughter would soon be gone from her. Having needed this time to allow her emotions to wash through her, Elysinia had gratefully conceded to being a careful listener. However, when the flow of the discussion naturally moved in her direction, she willingly contributed to the conversation.

Elysinia was both beautiful and kind. Her wisdom was respected and sought. When she finally spoke it was with grace and eloquence: "We have not been able to discern who or what it is. As Aolana mentioned, this one remains well-cloaked. He or she is no stranger to magic in its darker form. We believe it may be someone from your community," Elysinia looked in the direction of Ra-Ma'at, indicating that it was the Moon Clan to which she referred. She continued, "but...we don't know for sure."

Elysinia meant to assure the Moon Clan elders that it had not been the intention of the faeries to keep information from them. Nor had the Faery Council of Five suspected that any of those in attendance were involved. The Council of Five had just wanted to ascertain the truth before making any rash assumptions.

"I'll give you one guess who seems to be an obvious candidate, though!" The fiery faery elder blazed and burned. Sparks flew in every direction.

"Leori, that's enough. You don't know for sure. None of us do." Elysinia was fair, but firm. She wouldn't have anyone, especially not a council member, making speculations. "We are not going to gamble about something as serious as this."

Lunaya spoke up again, "We need to understand what we are dealing with. There is one way to learn the identity of the Dark One." An idea she had been toying with for days was finally stepping out from its hiding place. Like something that peeks in and out of shadowed spaces in one's imagination, this idea had crept around her thoughts, and yet it had not claimed for itself a spot in reality – until now. She knew what she was about to suggest was dangerous and, in most cases, seriously ill advised, if at all. Perhaps this was the very reason she had hesitated to allow it to gain a foothold in her repertoire of existing possibilities. Unflinchingly she delivered her proposition, which sounded more like a decision that had already been made: "I will journey to the Singing Mount."

A shiver carried by the winds rolled through the hearts of those present. Then an uncomfortable silence fell over the gathering. It loomed with a fierce intensity. Many screamed from within at the mere mention of the mountain.

It was Ra-Ma'at who broke the rising wave of tension with his objection to his sister's plan: "Lunaya...that journey is one best left alone. It is perilous and who knows how long it might take."

"Which is why I should leave at once. I realize it is not for the faint of heart. I'm not aware of another way. And I would rather know who, or what, we are up against." Lunaya was determined in this.

"I am going to come with you then," insisted Ra-Ma'at.

"No, Sonny. You must do what you came here to do." Ra-Ma'at softened at the use of his sister's nickname for him.

Lunaya looked at Elysinia, then back at her brother, "Stay and talk with Elysinia"

"Don't worry, Ra-Ma'at. I will go with Lunaya." It was Telzar, another of the Moon Clan Keepers that had attended this meeting of hearts. He'd been quiet and pensive, the whole time pondering deeply all that was being said. He was an obscure man, dark and mysterious. So deeply intense, he made many uncomfortable. This caused him to keep mostly to himself.

"And I shall accompany the both of you," Vayu blustered and blew. "The wind is, after all, my home, my friend, and my destiny. I know those parts well. And there may be someone there who knows them even better. Allow me to be your guide and faery envoy."

A loud cawing broke the tension. For the last two days the raven had remained perched on a nearby tree branch. While he seemed to have been listening to the human and faery interactions, it was hard to be sure. The bird was prone to wandering *between the worlds*. Either way he would have appeared to be physically present.

Many of the animals had been observing the gathering, but none had voiced an opinion one way or the other. The raven was the first one to speak. Yuri took flight and landed on Lunaya's shoulder.

"Take care, Keeper." The raven was genuine in his words. Yuri and Lunaya had grown quite fond of one another from working together over the last year. "It is quite unfortunate I will not be able to offer you any assistance in your mission this time. Summiting mountains is outside of my area of expertise, I'm afraid. Should you need a Messenger, however, you know how to reach me."

The bird was, after all, simply *one who walked between the worlds.* Lunaya saw the irony in the situation and smiled inside. How humorous that the bird could deliver a message to someone 13,000 years into the future, but that he did not climb or even fly on mountaintops. Then again at the altitude they were to be attempting she would be surprised if they found any life forms at all.

Ra-Ma'at started to object to the whole idea, but thought better of it. It was a brilliant plan – if they made it. The mountain was almost impossible to summit. "Please be careful," he whispered. Then he hugged his sister tightly. He turned to Telzar, "Look out for her." Telzar did not have a chance to answer. Lunaya had beaten him to it.

"Oh stop your worrying! You know I'll be fine. Besides Vayu will look out for both Telzar and me!" Lunaya placed her arms around Telzar and Vayu, one on either side of her. "Nothing is going to happen to this team!" They all laughed, all except for Vayu; he barely managed a smile, for he alone fully knew the risks involved with a journey to the Singing Mount. He had never known any humans to make the climb and live. This he decided not to mention.

****

The tiny gnome crouched by an old elderberry bush that obscured his presence. He didn't exactly intend to hide, but then he didn't mean to stand out, either. How interesting the affairs of humans and High Faeries could be. Jory hadn't traveled all this way to hear these tales – not really. He had made the journey with another intention in mind. He listened closely to the words they spoke about Rose's upcoming transformation, and he felt hope. Then their conversation turned to questions about darkness and Dark Ones, and his heart sank. The gnome slouched and his faced drooped long and low. He thought of the youngins and wondered what they would think of their father when they realized what he'd done. Worry creased his rosy cheeks and shame gripped his gut and wouldn't let go.

It was time to get a move on it, for while he knew these matters were of great importance, Jory had not made the long journey here to sit and listen to what was being discussed at the Great Gathering. The gnome slid away into the Forest unseen.

Chapter 6
Enter the Faery Mound

"The subterranean people [faeries] are linked to the land, each region having its counterpart in the underworld. Thus they are, in one respect, the genii loci of the ancient world."

- Robert Kirk, The Secret Commonwealth of Elves, Fauns & Fairies

The Forest – 11,000 BCE (3 weeks after the GG)

Strategies had been devised, and plans set into motion. Having been adjourned for several weeks, most had taken their leave from the Great Gathering. Not wanting to procrastinate, Lunaya, Telzar and Vayu had set out the day before. Elysinia approached Ra-Ma'at. She possessed such grace, as she floated on a moonlit cushion of water, wind and light. No words were spoken between them. Master Ra-Ma'at felt a peace come to settle within his heart. A whisper was heard there, "Everything will be all right." He didn't know if it was Elysinia or Peace itself that had spoken these words. Ultimately they were one and the same.

He thought of her daughter Rose, and what they meant to do: "Elysinia...I...I'm sorry I didn't understand at the time...," he trailed off, deeply affected by her warming smile that said neither an apology nor forgiveness was necessary.

She took his hand and they walked on. Understanding his desire to go to the Crystal Library, she led him toward a large mound just beyond the place where the Great Gathering had been held. He knew this was one of the many entrances to the Faery Realm. While the faeries didn't live beneath the Earth, where they existed was slightly beyond the physical plane.

Like a wand of light, her hand glowed brightly. Elysinia waved her hand over the rockier side of the mound. A passageway appeared. They stepped into the entrance. Then, just as soon as it had materialized, the passage disappeared to reveal nothing but a rocky mound once again.

Once inside, memories of the past began to rise up to the surface. Like a nostalgic wellspring, it surged the more deeply they moved within the Earth. Yet even in the midst of these intense emotions, the atmosphere was that of a nurturing womb welcoming them. If Life could wrap its arms around itself, then surely this was what it was doing, for that is how Ra-Ma'at felt as he moved deeper and deeper into the unknown.

As they continued on, the atoms around them shifted once again. The state of incubation was coming to an end, as one felt the final transition of walking from one world into another. Visible in the distance was a white light that grew and grew. The source of this luminescent radiance was unidentifiable; it was coming from everywhere.

Ra-Ma'at sensed a swirling bubbliness around them; like molecules rushing to mold substance, the energy began to form. Then suddenly they were in a world similar to the Forest they had just left behind but with an added depth that translated into the most vivid colors and pristine tones one could imagine. This world was one where colors, tones and vibrations were woven together creating beauty and harmony that surpassed description.

A world that existed on the inner planes of light came into focus. Waterfalls flowed from an azure sky. The thunderous cascades poured into crystalline pools of twinkling bands of colored light and billowed out like liquid rainbows that caressed the surrounding lands for miles around. A glorious forest kingdom stood before them. This kingdom consisted of loosely based open-air structures. In some places it was hard to tell where a tree ended and a wall began. The walls were gleaming and transparent, hewn from selenite and quartz. They served to create patterns of energy flow that supported peace, harmony and love.

Upon the walls were luscious vines that crept this way and that. Little bursts of color appeared everywhere in the form of flowers and their corresponding nature spirits. The ground rose up to meet them with moss-laden cushions as they walked. Approaching the entranceway of a great castle-like structure, they were greeted by two Earth Elves that flanked either side of the opening. The elves extended a proper faery greeting as was customary. Ra-Ma'at and Elysinia returned the gesture. Through the gates, they passed into the Kingdom of Faerie.

Side by side they walked on silently, content within one another's presence. It was amazing how so much had been so important to say only days ago. Now nothing was really that important. Ra-Ma'at wasn't focused on the past any longer, nor was he worried about the future. Somehow he knew all would be well – somehow walking here next to her made him certain.

When Elysinia spoke it was like a summer breeze that gently carried bits of sweet fragrance: "Ra-Ma'at, we are close now to the Crystal Library. I understand the reason you wish to visit. You have come for the Prophecy Egg that you bequeathed to our collection so long ago."

"Yes, the crystal that holds the Dragon Clan's most treasured secret…and…."

Elysinia smiled in understanding, encouraging him to continue. Ra-Ma'at still blamed himself for Taivyn leaving.

In a comforting voice that sounded like a lullaby she said, "Ra-Ma'at, you mustn't blame yourself. Do not worry over the boy. The Forest listens and tells us its stories, you know. Having heard your plea for help, he will be looked after."

Ra-Ma'at was surprised, "He's all right, then? Oh thank the Great Spirit."

"He is fine, yes. He has a quest of his own, however. I believe a part of you has known that. Isn't that after all why you truly seek the prophecy? Let me assure you he is not only the Silver Prince, but also the last of the Dragon clan."

Chapter 7
The Crystal Library

"The only terms that ever satisfied me as describing Nature are the terms used in fairy books, charm, spell, enchantment. They express the arbitrariness of the fact and its mystery."

- G.K. Chesterton

Somewhere in Faerie - timeless

Hearing her say the words aloud had produced a shiver through his entire body that he had not expected. A screenplay of memories rolled through his heart: a baby in a basket brought to him by a faery emissary; the dreams that the boy started having shortly after his sixteenth birthday; Taivyn's uncanny connection to horses; little clues that had been there all along. So much had he accepted the boy as part of the community that perhaps he had been blind to the signs. Maybe a part of him had always known. How could he have been so ignorant?

"You knew…you've always known?" Ra-Ma'at questioned.

"Yes. And I suspect that if you look deep within yourself, you'll realize you did, too."

"Yes, I suppose I did."

Just then they arrived at the Crystal Library. In the middle of the cavern, and sufficing as a table, a large flat stone rose up from the ground. Filled with maps of stars, it stood in the center of this vast room. Crystals of all shapes and colors lined the walls of the cavern. Ra-Ma'at looked up at the skylight, a detail most of the underground caverns in the Faery Kingdom possessed. The beauty of the night sky poured into the space, illuminating it. The stars corresponded with the crystals in a constant dialogue of truth and light. His memory had not served him well, for the splendor of this place far surpassed his recollection.

Contented to know how much pleasure he took in visiting this library, Elysinia walked over to where a large ledge held ancient written works. The room was filled with such ledges. Projecting out of the walls, they were structures of woven silvery reeds that were shelf-like in function.

Large stalactites grew from the ceiling like icicles, streaming violet and indigo hues. Quartz and amethyst protruded from the ground in fractal patterns holding within their matrices ancient stories, and a labyrinthine path wound its way through these living records of time, providing a walkway for visitors to this place. Ra-Ma'at circled the room in reverence and wonder. He marveled at the many new editions – crystals suspended in the air that awaited their perfect placement among the other records; Elysinia had been busy.

While the crystals made up the medium of storage for the majority of the records within this library, it was plentiful with scrolls, too. Reaching into a glass case that stood beside one of the ledges, Elysinia produced one rolled up and secured with a ribbon forged in moonlight. When she returned to the center of the room, she gently released the scroll. Instead of falling, it gently floated, suspended in midair, and unfurled itself, then rested softly atop the round stone table. Ra-Ma'at looked at her questioningly.

"A scroll? I don't understand. Where is the Prophecy Egg?"

"Somewhere safe."

"But what could be safer than here?"

"I returned it long ago to its true owner."

"But I thought you said Taivyn was the last."

"He is," she paused. Then she sighed before adding, "But he wasn't always."

Chapter 8
Dreams and Dragons

"Faeries are not a fantasy but a connection to reality."

-Brian Froud, *Good Faeries, Bad Faeries*

The Forest – 11,000 BCE (3 months after GG)

The tail moved beneath the earth's surface. It was big and bold as it dreamed the dream of the Earth. The sacred Dreamtime was made for dragons and dragons made for it. Dragons were both Movers and Dreamers. They lay sleeping now on the Inner Earth. Where they were exactly, no one knew.

Once a proud race flying and gliding through the skies, now they had retreated to the Inner Realms, for safety and providence. They could no longer sustain on the surface. Too dense was the air and light, they could not abide there, no.

A dragon stirred deep in the Earth now. Its long tail stretched miles and miles. The small subterranean gnomes bounced around its great length helping the stones below. Somewhere in the dark subterranean depths grew a smallish plant. Its leaves were oval shaped emeralds and its thorns delicate yet sharp. From its sepal burst a small bud almost igniting into blossom. A tiny red bud.

S till relishing in the warmth of the Inner Earth, Taivyn awoke mildly disoriented as he suddenly became acutely aware of the contrast of cold ground upon which he lay. He thought of heading inside to give himself a reprieve from the damp chill. The cottage was stone-faced and a tiny stream of smoke poured from its red rock chimney. Conjuring up the images of his dream, he realized he must have fallen asleep in the middle of the day once again.

Why am I doing this so often now?

Sometimes out of nowhere he would just go completely out cold. A few times he'd even done so while standing up. He shook himself off before going inside. Dried up leaves and grasses fell from his britches and tunic. He surely couldn't remember the last time he'd bathed. Perhaps he should see to that. The seasons had taken a turn. This was the time of year that the weather usually started to warm. However, it seemed to be getting darker and colder. Taivyn wondered if the moon would be out tonight. The haziness of the clouds sure made it difficult to see.

He pushed through the little door – a half oval piece of wood colored red just like the chimney.

****

The old woman sat brewing her hot concoction over the fire. Hanging above the conflagration, a cauldron bubbled and oozed, delighted to be stirred so attentively. Every now and then a spark, a flash of fizzle, would jump from its place below demonstrating that it, too, could be brave and bold by stepping out into the world. Of course just like all things that step out into the world before their time, the cinder was soon reduced to nothing but a cold black ash that vanished with the first gusty draught from the window.

Content to leave her cauldron brew and toil alone for a while, she hobbled over to the window where a family of black squirrels awaited her generosity. The old woman offered them a few crumbles from the recently baked loaf of brown bread. The unexpected cold was challenging the food supply, and the Forest creatures were in need of sustenance.

While such a seemingly small amount, the bits of bread meant mountains to these animals. The squirrels relished in the warm heart that doted on them. To find companionship in one outside of the Animal Kingdom was rare these days. Gratefully gobbling their crumbs, they chirped and crunched, all the while nuzzling gently the hand that fed them.

On the other side of the cottage, and over in the far window, a smallish being climbed up to have a look inside.

But nothing went unseen by the old woman. No sooner had the creature plopped down to make itself comfortable, and she was en route, slowly making her way over.

"Fine Day to you, Wallen!"

Wallen tipped his tiny, pointed yellow hat in greeting, as he was unable to speak due to the large quantity of nuts he had just inhaled. "What is this, feeding time for everyone?" Amelda remarked more to herself than to anyone in particular.

Swallowing hard and loudly, Wallen felt inclined to answer, "I should think gnomes are the only beings who've designated a 'sepper' time. That being said, I suppose others may eat around this time if they choose. In fact, I shouldn't see a reason why everyone does not...."

Wallen trailed off thoughtfully, having apparently stumped himself with this line of mental musing.

"Wallen?" A sharp gaze was all the prompting the gnome required to nudge his memory.

"Yes, right. Amelda, I haven't found him yet," was Wallen's answer.

Gnomes! Must they leave everything to the imagination?

"How does a gnome simply vanish?" Amelda was incredulous.

"Yes, well, the Grandfather is quite interested to know that, too," Wallen was slightly nervous. Gnomes were predictable, after all. And that this one wasn't, was all too chaotic for his taste.

"And no one has seen him?" Amelda wanted to know.

"Not since the last Great Gathering, almost three moons ago," Wallen assured her.

A nervous trickle crept into her otherwise serene temperament. "And you're sure he has it?"

"Well, yes. He was the last to be seen with it, apparently." Wallen was just as stumped as she.

"But why would he take it? It just doesn't make any sense." Amelda was having difficultly not letting the worry take over.

"Perhaps he thought it needed a polish, and...," Wallen could see his efforts to lighten the mood fell upon deaf ears. Amelda looked uncharacteristically distressed. The gnome wondered aloud, "Do you need it?"

Then suddenly the little red half oval of a door flung open.

"Amelda!" Taivyn called

Amelda scuttled from the window and back over to the cauldron to observe the brew's progress. "Yes, dear. Over here. I'm just preparing a bite for us. Some brown bread and nuts with a bit of rabbit. Sit down there and warm yourself by the fire."

"All right."

Amelda peered over at him. She eyed him suspiciously. "Taivyn, something wrong?"

Taivyn sighed, "No...yes...no, not really. It's just that I had another one of those dreams."

She raised her eyebrows, "Oh...do tell, dear."

"I don't know. It's not much different than the last ones. Only I feel like they are more real now. As if I'm actually there."

The old woman looked deeply concerned, although he didn't know why. "How about I make you a nice draught of tea tonight. That should help you to have a dreamless sleep. At least for one night."

"I don't know. I guess that would be nice." She had become like a mother to him, only she was old enough to be his grandmother.

"All right, well, just relax then."

Taivyn sighed, "I just wish I understood."

While she was endeared to the boy for saving her life, she couldn't risk sharing the truth unless she were absolutely certain. However, the dreams were proof enough, were they not? A cause, at least, to wonder if perhaps he were just the one she maintained her silence for in the first place. Surely she would have recognized him, though. And she did not, not in the slightest. She would not make another mistake again, however, for a price had been demanded that she was still paying.

They ate their supper and relaxed by the fire.

"You think we might be able to see the moon tonight?"

Amelda got up to peer out the window. She drew the drape back and looked out. "I'm afraid not, my dear. Clouds are heavy."

"Well, then, I'm going to turn in a little early tonight. Would that be all right?"

"Of course, dear."

Taivyn peeled himself off the fur-covered chair and bumbled into the little cove. He drew the folds of fabric to create a private enclosure. The pallet was several layers thick, and easy to become quite comfortable in. Since leaving the Moon Clan community he had certainly slept in a lot worse. Sometimes he couldn't believe it had been almost three months since that day. He wondered if he had made the right choice. Determined was he to complete his quest to find out who he was. Yet sometimes, just sometimes, he missed them. He missed the Master and Korin. Even some of his fellow apprentices were worth missing. He couldn't turn back now – not before he had answers, anyway.

He thought again about the person he was when he had started his quest. He had been no one. That's how it had felt anyway. He hadn't known who he was, or where he had come from. Then he had met Jedda. That's when everything had changed. Looking into her eyes, it was like the secrets to his soul might be revealed at any moment. He still hadn't gotten any concrete answers, but something about simply being with her informed him of the deepest truth of who he was. And just who was she? She had said her name was Jedda, but who was she really? And where had she gone?

People don't just vanish into thin air, he told himself.

But she did. A part of him had known that she wasn't coming back, while the other part didn't know how he could get on without her. He had felt at odds with himself about the whole thing. He couldn't explain it now any more than he could then. Since beginning his so-called quest there were a lot of things he couldn't explain. Taivyn thought about all this for a while. Before too long he was fast asleep.

Amelda waited to hear a light snore before rising from her seat. She set her teacup down in the basin to be washed a little later. Right now something else ruled her attention. She walked across the little cottage and over to the front door. She gave one more listen to make sure Taivyn was asleep. Then she stepped out. The sky was crystal clear. Stars could be seen across the firmament, and a falling sparkle here and there. The moon hung low and was a crescent this night. Amelda sighed. She didn't like lying to the boy. But then certain things couldn't be helped.

****

Somewhere Else in The Forest

Something was amiss in the Forest. A dark presence had been brewing for weeks, months, even years. The greed that had begun to ensnare the hearts of men stoked its fire. As their lights started to dim, it grew stronger.

He peered down at the oval-shaped crystal that lay quivering and crying before him. It had found its way to him unwillingly, sold into slavery for a pittance. Gnomes! Always willing to trade anything, even a crystal, for someone they care about. And this wasn't just any crystal. Fool! What a fool! And a good thing for that, because it had worked out advantageously, for now he had what he needed – The Prophecy Egg.

The Dark One grabbed the crystal tightly. The crystal cringed. It detested being in the clutches of such a tainted heart. If only it hadn't been broken…it could have sent out a cry for help.

Chapter 9
Legends Come Alive

*"Seers and visionaries receive feedback
from their ambient surroundings and
conditions, though they perceive also what lies
beyond the feth-fiadha [the veil]."*

– Caitlin Matthews, *Celtic Visions*

Maine – 1976

"The Wheel of the Ages is turning once again, Dear Ones," the elder woman spoke with grace and power. Gray eyes flashed within a tender face that had seen more than even her years would suggest.

"Yes, Grandmother. I know. We have waited a long time for this." A grandmother by blood she was not. However the title was used to denote a certain level of both respect and wisdom.

"Yes, and we must be sure it is not in vain. You know that the dragons must finally awaken."

The young woman was in just as much shock as were her two male companions. "How can it be? Then it is more than just an ancient prophecy...."

"Isn't it always?" Oftentimes the Grandmother spoke in code, but tonight she was being as clear as ever.

"How can you be sure?" questioned one of the young men, although he regretted his doubt-filled question as soon as it had left his mouth. His grim manner made the air in the atmosphere stand still.

"Malin, I am quite surprised at you," was the Grandmother's only reply. The old woman moved on, turning her attention to the young woman.

"The dragons cannot sleep through another age. The Earth will not make it without them."

"What can we do to help?" asked the other male companion. While he wasn't yet a man of thirty, his prematurely greying hair and beard added at least ten years of age to his chiseled appearance.

Now the Grandmother turned to him directly, "Sonny, we must find the Silver One."

11,000 BCE

Not yet emerged from the red egg of fire, the mother guarded them with all her love and all her might. Flames still licked this oval mass – a ball of moving light with reds and oranges that danced across its surface. Located in the forgotten and fiery depths, these unhatched family additions grew in strength and size and waiting. On many levels they were already far beyond the consciousness of many creatures that inhabited the Earth. When born they did not begin anew. Instead their wisdom was passed down from eon to eon, and was ancestral in nature. Collected over time as it was by their kind, each newly born already owned in consciousness that which its ancestors had learned and understood. Their wisdom was ancient and collective, and so were they.

The dragons lay sleeping beneath the Earth's surface. Each age was governed by a particular dragon – until the Age of Light, which would be governed by all.

Maine – 2005

"It is time now, my child. I wish to meet the girl. I'd like to see for myself."

The Grandmother stood in the Great Hall, talking softly to Lou on her phone. The Great Hall was located just beyond the temple entrance. This proud building had stood for more than a century. It hadn't always been a temple. It wasn't until the 1970s that the Moon Clan had procured the space. While it had been quite elaborate at the time, they had added their own embellishments over the last several decades. Now it acted as the North American headquarters for the Order.

"Of course, but I have already determined she is the one – to be trained in the path of the Initiate – the next Keeper. Is there something more?" Lou asked. A twinge of insecurity colored her otherwise unyielding confidence in her intuition.

Does she not trust my judgment? Lou wondered to herself.

There was a momentary pause. Then the Grandmother responded, "As a matter of fact there is. Do you remember when I spoke to you about the dragons many years ago?"

The answer had both surprised and relieved Lou. "Well, yes, of course. You said that it was imperative that they awaken for the Turning of the Ages this time. But we never spoke of it again. Why do you bring it up now?" Lou grew curious. She knew the Grandmother well enough to know that she never kindled a conversation unnecessarily.

"Lou, why don't we meet this evening? There is something I want to ask you about." The last thing Lou had time for was another meeting. This was a busy time of the year with Spring break just around the corner. She would not think to decline, however. The Grandmother was the woman who had taught her everything she knew, and then some. She was also her aunt.

"Should I come to the Moon Clan temple then, Aunt Elda? I could meet you in the faery gardens?" Lou offered, hoping to make it as effortless on herself as possible. She could easily swing by there based on the proximity of the temple to both her home and school. The Grandmother had another idea.

"I think not. Do you remember the sacred well? The one I used to take you to as a child?"

"Why yes, of course. The spring that never runs dry. The one that flows under the sacred oak tree." Lou remembered it well.

"Yes. I will see you there at sundown," the elder confirmed.

Chapter 10
By the Water

"The heart of Nature, save for its rhythmic pulse, abides in silence. The devotee at Nature's shrine must approach her altar reverently and with quiet mind if he would find her beating heart and know the power within the form."

- Geoffrey Hodson, *The Kingdom of the Gods*

Maine – 2005

The sacred oak tree filtered the light of the setting sun like stained glass. Shimmering light reflected off the waters of the spring that flowed just beneath the ancient tree. Lou sat near to the fount, patiently waiting for her aunt to join her. She placed her long delicate hands into the cool, healing waters. No one knew how long the spring had been there. The early settlers spoke of its healing powers, but even before them there were mentions of it that circulated in the legends of the Natives.

Lou's golden hair sparkled in the sun's orange fire. Water droplets fell upon her forehead and lips as she brought her hands to her face, drizzling the water ever so carefully. She loved the effect this spring had upon her mood. She had not come here in a while and didn't realize until now how much she had missed it.

Sweet singing preceded the sound of soft footsteps indicating someone was approaching by way of the Western footpath. The Grandmother's silver strands of hair bounced softly over her shoulders as she made her way to where Lou rested. The old woman sat down and smiled at her niece.

"It's beautiful, isn't it?" the Grandmother gazed at the surrounding landscape of hills and trees outlined by the grey sea in the distance.

"Yes. It is. I used to love coming here."

"Perhaps you can find the time once again. It heals, you know."

Lou did know. The tingling sensations that moved through her body as a result of spending time in this place were profoundly peaceful and soothing. After taking it all in for a few more minutes, Lou decided to cut to the chase.

"So why have you asked me here?"

"Ah, Lou, always in a hurry." Her aunt smiled at her. "Have you spoken to Sonny Ramen lately?"

"Why, no. We see each other in passing, of course. But I have barely had time for anything as of late. Between my students and working with Jedda, it leaves little time for socializing."

"Is that what you call coming together and sharing with your soul siblings?"

The Grandmother chuckled. She liked to give Lou a hard time once in a while. They had always had a close relationship. Quite frankly, she wished they were closer these days. She knew that the search for the next Keeper had been very taxing for Lou. All that was behind her now, though. There was no reason why she couldn't lighten up a bit, and spend some time in community. Living alone and thinking alone and figuring things out alone wasn't all that healthy. One needed friends; one needed family. She wished sometimes that Lou would lean on her for support. Lou had always wanted to show her how capable she was, only she hadn't needed to prove that. The Grandmother knew very well how capable the woman was.

Lou had looked dismayed at the Grandmother's comment. "Lou, I am only joking with you. Where has your sense of humor gotten off to?"

Lou couldn't help feeling a little vulnerable, "I'm sorry, Aunt Elda."

"That's all right, dear. You know how much I love you. I mean nothing by my jesting," she patted her hand reassuringly. "About Sonny though. I think you might do well to pay him a visit. He has been working on something very important and his theories may be quite interesting to you."

Lou nodded. She realized then that she really had distanced herself. She and Sonny hadn't talked in months. And she certainly had no idea what he had been working on as of late. If she knew Sonny, he'd wrestle with it until he had it sorted out, whatever it was. He was determined and steadfast, dedicated to his work and commitment to spiritual evolution. He was also dedicated to his students, both the ones at school as well as the nontraditional ones.

"Something to do with his apprentices maybe?" Sonny handled all the instruction for the Moon Clan overflow that Lou could not get to. They tried to make their teaching as uniform as possible.

"Not entirely. We'll see, though."

Lou thought she'd take the opportunity to ask the Grandmother something that had been weighing on her.

"Why didn't you tell me about Artemis? You knew he had left…why didn't you let me know?"

"I wanted everything to occur naturally. I knew you would find her. And you have."

"But if Artemis has left you, then that means…." Tears came into Lou's eyes. While the Grandmother had not been in an active role for some time, she was still technically the eldest Keeper; once a Keeper, always a Keeper.

"Yes, dear. Soon. But we have always known that this day would come."

Lou threw her arms around her aunt, and cried. "I love you, Aunt Elda. I don't want you to leave me."

The Grandmother hugged her tightly. "I love you, too, dear. And you know I will always be with you."

Lou, of course, knew the natural order of things. That didn't make it easy. Lou had always relied on her aunt being there if she had needed her even if she made herself come across as self-sufficient. Lou dried her eyes.

"I know, Aunt Elda. I know."

Lou got up to leave. She brushed herself off. She knelt down one more time. She touched the running waters. Peace and tranquility flooded her body and mind. She kissed her aunt on the forehead.

"I will find time to talk with Sonny. Perhaps this weekend. Tomorrow Jedda and I will be over to your house in the afternoon. We will drop by after school for tea, is that okay?"

"That's fine, dear."

"Okay, I've got to go. I will see you tomorrow." As Lou turned to walk away, the Grandmother quickly added, "Oh and Lou, one more thing." She paused to make sure she had Lou's attention, "I think it may be time for you to take a little trip."

Chapter 11
The Grandmother

"...[the seers] know that the spiritual and emotional meaning of life is not found just on one shore of reality, but is brought to us by the tides originating on the further shore, by way of dream, and impressions that we tend to neglect as irrational promptings of no account. What if we were to live as if that dialogue were the truest thing we ever did?"

-Caitlin Matthews, *Celtic Visions*

Maine – 2005

The floors creaked when walked upon, announcing the presence of humans and mice alike. Yuck! The thought of mice running freely around at night made Jedda's skin crawl. The creatures were cute enough when contained properly, but scampering through one's home freely was cause for nervousness. Oh well. If it didn't bother the old woman, she supposed it didn't really matter.

Jedda sat upon a lavishly upholstered love seat dating from the late 1800s. Of European origin, most probably French, it was richly laden in deep purple and fuchsia hues. Not tasteless, however; the design was surprisingly alluring, pleasing to the eyes.

She took a sip of tea from the small china teacup that rested perfectly in its matching saucer – a delicate antique of porcelain white with gold trim. Staring up at the old wooden boards that made up the walls of this turn-of-the-century little house, she wondered what experiences this woman had lived to tell.

A painting that had adorned these walls for who knows how long caught her eye. She'd been drawn to it from the moment they arrived. It evoked a deep and growing emotion. A harmonious medley of light and shadow, the piece perfectly conveyed a dreamlike state. Jedda sat entranced. Was the artist expressing his or her own feelings through this work or was he or she relating a deeper message? Perhaps they were attempting to portray the mystery of the place in the painting. Languid blues gave way to swirling orchids that made up the twilight sky. The large and leering hill that protruded in the background was somehow the focal point of this landscape even though it took up so little of the actual canvas. An erect and lonely tower rose from out of the mound's precipice that gave way to a shadowy and eerie light. While it was easy enough to distinguish the light originated from somewhere behind this tower, the source remained uncannily unknown.

"No matter how many times I stare at that painting it never gets old. Sometimes it even seems to change. The view is always the same, but the light...the light seems alive." The Grandmother had a sparkle in her eye.

"Perhaps it is the sunlight that comes from your windows that gifts the painting with such an interesting effect. A trick of the light on the eyes...," Jedda chuckled nervously. Although trying to rationalize the Grandmother's observation of the painting, somehow she knew there was no reasoning for the emotional effect she felt.

As if the Grandmother knew this, she said, "Yes, dear. You could perhaps make a case for that. But I think you and I know there is more to it than meets the eye, hmm...?"

"But Grandmother Elda, what is it? I mean is it a real place?"

"But of course it is, dear. And it is known as the Avalantia Tor."

"The Tor..." The word rolled off of Jedda's lips, betraying a hint of nostalgia. The hill was hypnotic by its very nature, and as Jedda sat there, gaze unbroken, a reverberating tone rose up from within her. Jedda's heart vibrated gently in her chest, chanting an unknown hymn. Then she saw the chamber. It was only for a fleeting second, but it flashed clear as day within the painting. There was a hidden chamber within this sacred hill. No sooner had she blinked then it was gone. Jedda gasped aloud. Eyes wide, she whirled around, and stared questioningly at the Grandmother.

Smiling, the Grandmother nodded reassuringly. "As I said, it changes. Perhaps it was the sunlight, dear."

"Grandmother, you and I both know that what I just saw was not the sunlight."

"Well, you don't say." The Grandmother just continued smiling. However, her eyes were shining with something much closer to satisfaction. Just then Lou walked into the room with another pot of tea, "More tea anyone? It's piping hot and has just finished steeping." Lou walked over to where the empty teacups sat upon the baroque coffee table. As she reached over to refill her aunt's cup, the old woman met her gaze.

"Let us discuss the trip I mentioned earlier, shall we?" the Grandmother said.

Chapter 12
The Dark Gathering

"...in the time when the divine race and the human race and the soulless race and the dumb races that are near to man were all one race."

– Fiona Macleod, *The Winged Destiny*

Maine – 2005

To the outsider, the structure looked abandoned and dilapidated. Little more than a skeleton of metal beams, deteriorated joists and rafters were all that seemed to remain. A dark figure in a trench coat moved through the outer edges. He stomped and twisted his way through the rotting and termite-infested boards. The less life that it displayed the better. It drew less attention that way. He walked over to some metal piping that spit out of the ground. To any passersby this was an old drainpipe in disuse for decades. The dark one had known that these air ducts would come in handy. He walked deliberately over to the far wall. A small and nearly hidden lever rested near to the ground. He pulled it and waited. Then part of the floor slid away to reveal a large opening in the ground. He reached inside his long coat and pulled out a flashlight. Turning it on to illuminate the large set of stairs that descended before him, he stepped down into the opening. Then he disappeared. The floor slid back over the opening to disguise the entryway once again.

Under the old warehouse was where he worked and mostly lived. He had a formal residence above ground, but it was mostly for show; he rarely spent any time there. The boys gathered round as they had for years. This was their domain. They were happy to be free of their parents' strict rules and teachings for a short while. They were happy to actually learn something real.

"The time is approaching when you will need to use that which I have taught you," the dark figure hissed.

Gus, the oldest boy, spat and scowled.

The dark figure just smiled and thought to himself, *He has come along nicely*. Darkness was the way. It had always been the way. And soon that way was going to get a lot longer.

The youngest boy of the bunch, Joel, groaned, "Well, I sure do hope this ain't like high school algebra, or sentence diagramming." Joel let out another loud growl before finishing his thought, "Dammit! Mr. Ramen always has us doing things we'll never use in life. I keep asking, 'Why do I need this?' What a waste of time."

The dark man grimaced. He knew that professor. He knew him well. And he did not like his name spoken around him, especially not here, in his domain.

"I'm am nothing like that pathetic professor! Don't you dare compare me to the likes of him! You watch your tongue, Joel. Do not cross me!" the dark man snarled.

Within his eyes a storm appeared to be brewing; his irises appeared to bulge in response to the boy's whining. This was enough to rattle even Gus who up until then had been little more than bored. The dark man reigned them in like fiercely trained dogs that pulled a sled. All he had to do was crack the whip and they were set to obey. They knew better. And they had no choice.

"I'm sorry, Malin," Joel just barely managed to stammer.

He had been culling them for years. An after-school program for lost boys was how they spun it. Malin presented himself as a coach who was interested in helping at-risk young men turn their lives around before it was too late. A coach indeed. He knew what these boys needed. They needed to feel empowered and useful. Well, power they would feel moving through their fingertips. He would see to that. You had to give them something to keep them tethered like junkies. String them along, until their usefulness ran out.

He'd been very particular with who was to be solicited for this "program," as he called it. Trial and error over long periods made it very clear that reward comes from careful selection and proper instruction.

More like brainwashing. Whatever it was, it worked. Break them down. Then build them up as you would like. They needed to be fit to serve. And serve they would.

Misfit children of the Moon Clan had always been his focus until he had come across....

He looked around. One, two, three, four, five...someone was missing...a roar split the air. The dragon that had been sleeping within him suddenly awoke; it could forget about ever escaping. Nothing escaped. Not from Malin! Not ever.

Gus stood shaking in his boots. Malin turned to him like a wolf that had just locked onto its prey. When Malin opened his mouth to speak it was like a steam engine had blown, and the whole subterranean structure around them might collapse: "Where is Vyncent?!"

Chapter 13
The Waters Speak

"The plant nation is the green-blooded kingdom...
a kingdom without karma, for karma
begins with red blood."

– Ann Manser, *Shustah*

The Forest – 11,000 BCE (3 months after GG)

The dragons slept and dreamed. They waited.
They waited to be called. Waited to be
summoned. By the one who was bound to them
by blood and spirit. The boy slept and the boy
dreamed. He held within his hands the silvery
egg-shaped crystal. The Prophecy Egg. The
Prophecy would be fulfilled.

Amelda scurried through the night and into the
Forest. Over on the far Northern edge of the land,
about a ten-minute walk from her cottage, was a well.
Taivyn had once asked if he could get water out of it

instead of walking to the river. She persuaded him against it without much explanation as to why. He seemed disappointed, but the boy tended to get over things quickly.

Amelda grabbed the small wooden pail that hung from a rope and lowered it down. She heard it plop into the water far down below. She worked hard to raise it back again. Sweating and nearly out of breath, she finally pulled the pail back into place. She placed a small silver goblet inside to draw some of the water she had collected.

"What could the boy's dreams mean?"

She held the water up to her lips to take a sip. Could it really be him…could he be her…?

"Fancy finding you here."

"Rose, I didn't expect to see you this night. To what do I owe the honor?"

Rose had appeared out of nowhere and startled Amelda. She hadn't expected to find anyone here, least of all the Record Keeper's daughter. Staring expectantly at the faery, she wondered what she might want. What entrancing beauty this creature before her possessed – silvery white skin and hair that would make rubescent silk appear dull in comparison. The starlight that radiated from her skin befitted her inner beauty and grace. The trees quivered with delight at the sound of Rose's voice, a melodious tune that ushered forth like flowers singing to one another.

"My mother has asked me to visit you to ensure you still have the Prophecy Egg," Rose said matter-of-factly. Amelda detected the slightest hint of concern beneath that cool, even tone. It had been over forty years since the faery's mother, Elysinia, had returned it to her, and never had she enquired after it once.

"I have placed it in the hands of those who guard crystals with their lives." Amelda did not offer the recent news of its unknown whereabouts.

"The gnomes...but why would you...?"

Amelda interrupted, answering the question before Rose could finish: "It was no longer safe here."

The old woman thought back on the error her poor judgment had resulted in all those years ago. How could she have known his heart might turn in such a way? But rumors brought by the winds of the Forest did not lie. She sighed as she thought of what had become of him, her own nephew.

Then she turned her thoughts to the young boy who abided with her now at the cottage. She did not dare mention him to Rose; she needed to be certain before stirring the young faery's longing heart. Amelda was acutely aware of the history between the faery and the young man that Amelda thought Taivyn might be.

"Amelda. Why do you drink now? You know that these waters give, but they also take."

Amelda knew all too well. Her years were upon her now. And because of her thirst for knowledge she might not see another moon. But she had to know! She had to know what connection the boy might have to that which she had spent her life guarding, and if somehow it was possible if...no, she mustn't get ahead of herself. Not yet. Not now. She gazed at the goblet before her. Perhaps the waters would shed some light. Well, then it would all be worth it, now wouldn't it? Amelda chuckled.

"What do you find so humorous?" Rose asked curiously.

"I was just thinking about life really. I believe life is humorous," Amelda stated candidly.

Rose was thoughtful. Then answered, "Yes, I suppose it is. Beautiful. Humorous. Wonderful. Yes...," Rose started to say something more, then hesitated.

"What is it? What troubles you?" Amelda asked with a genuineness that deeply touched the faery.

Rose dared not speak of it. "I...I am sorry. I am unable to share what it is I feel at this time. It's a jumble really, and..."

Amelda understood. Some things were best left alone. She'd learned that long ago. Perhaps if she had understood that in her earlier years.... But no matter.

"I understand," Amelda said.

"I'm sorry I must be going. Please forgive me for not being able to stay. I trust the gnomes will ensure the prophecy's safety until the time is right."

Amelda nodded. Rose slid off into the trees and shrubs. Only a trail of soft glowing light remained where she once stood. Then it, too, was gone. The old woman looked to the goblet. She paused momentarily before going ahead. Then she brought the silver cup to her mouth. She knew she wouldn't make it through this last imbibing. But she was almost sure she'd make it until morning. Taivyn would surely find her and then in her last moments she could tell him if he were indeed the one she was almost sure she believed him to be. *Tell me, I must know about the boy.* Then she drank.

The old woman fell back and crashed on the Forest floor. The goblet fell from her hands onto the ground beside her. She lay there in the grass, gasping. This time would be her last. This time the waters would finally take her soul across the eternal sea. The time had come.

****

The morning came and brought with it the sun that shone through the fabric. Taivyn stirred. He felt the warmth of its light on his skin. He popped up, excited that the dreariness had finally passed. *No more clouds,* he thought to himself.

"Amelda! Amelda! Wake up. The clouds are finally gone. The sun has come out to greet us."

He walked into her tiny room. She wasn't there. *She must already be up enjoying this blessed morning*, he thought. *Let's go see if we can find her.* He grabbed a green cloak. The air was still brisk. *Can't let the sun fool you.* It had been quite chilly in the mornings. He strolled out the front door and started calling for her. He didn't see her in the front. She must have gone a ways into the Forest to look for berries and nuts. Having lived with her almost a full season, he knew his way around by now. *Where has she gotten off to?*

Then he wondered if she'd gone down by that old well. She seemed to like it there. She always stayed gone for a while when she made her trips to that place.

Must be all the wonderful wildflowers and nature spirits around the area. He made his way over rather hurriedly, anxious to catch up with her this morning. When he came within eyesight of the old structure he stopped short. No!

"Amelda! Amelda!" he rushed to her side. Please, please don't let him be too late. Please.

"Amelda! Amelda!"

"Taivyn, my dear," the old lady managed. "I knew you would come."

"Amelda, what's happened? How can I help? I need to get you inside to administer one of your teas like you showed me last time." He started to lift her.

She feebly lifted her hand in a gesture that said to stop. Taivyn looked confused and scared. Amelda felt sad. She didn't want to leave him. He'd been abandoned too much in his short life, she knew that now. The grief of her past decision weighed heavy on her dying heart.

"Taivyn, there isn't any time. I'm sorry, but I had to."

Taivyn saw the goblet that lay beside the old woman he had come to love like the grandmother he'd never had.

"What's happened? What did you drink? You know the Forest so well. You wouldn't make a mistake…"

"Taivyn, I don't have much time left. I need to tell you. I know why you are having the dreams. And if what I have seen is true then you're in grave danger."

Taivyn didn't know what she was talking about. How could she have learned what the dreams meant when just yesterday she didn't know?

"My dear, your destiny has always been great. But the danger is greater. You are who the prophecy speaks of – you are…the last."

She was weak and could barely speak now.

"The last what?"

"The last…," Amelda faded. Her head dropped. "The last of the dragon clan."

Then with her last breath: "I'm sorry to leave you, my boy. I'm sorry to leave you…again."

Again? What does she mean?

"Amelda, no! Don't leave me. Please don't leave. Please. Tell me what to do!" He was screaming, as if his railing would change this outcome here and now.

But it was too late. Amelda was gone.

Chapter 14
Guardians of the Earth

"For it is one of their [the faeries] Tenets, That nothing perishes, but as the Sun and [the] Year, everything goes [around] in a Circle, Lesser or Greater, and is renewed, and refreshed in its revolutions. And it is another [tenet] that Every Body in the Creation moves, which [movement] is a sort of life, and that nothing moves but has another Animal moving on it, and so on, to the utmost minute corpuscle that is capable to be a receptacle of Lyfe."

- Robert Kirk, *The Secret Commonwealth of Elves, Fauns & Fairies*

26,000 years ago (13,000 before GG)

*T*hey rolled through the land unbounded. As the First Guardians of the Earth, they knew her intimately. Without the dragons, balance could not be. In a position of rest, they would not often be found, for it was their motion that kept the balance. They glided and rolled low to the ground, and at times, and when conditions required, they graced the sky with their soaring presence. Their place in the great design was so revered. All knew the significance of their existence, for without the dragons, chaos would ensue. Harmony is forward motion within divine will. And so it was in the days of old.

Fiery creatures some, watery creatures others. Creatures that contained within them swirling energies made of the elements. They glided over the land in graceful lunges, rings of fire, twirling light. A dazzling show of color. The Red Dragon bounded through the fields and just over the Forest canopy. Like burning red cinders, her scales blinked in and out of time. A whirling dervish in flight, she was the leader of the Fire coven.

The Dragons belonged to no one, and no one to them. They were protectors of the land, stewards, but they did not throw their weight around. And they did not take power lightly.

Over time the Dragons went to sleep. They retreated deep within the Earth. They would not leave the Earth, they would not abandon her, but they would retreat deep within to the Inner Planes. And in their place they would leave those who knew and honored them. Those who knew them so well that they would house within their bodies a way to summon the dragons to the Earth's surface if the need should ever arise. To call these ones humans would not be entirely accurate. Yet Fae they were not. Nay, they were something else altogether. Something magical and something in between. And as time went on they came together in a coven of their own and came to be known as the Dragon Clan.

Chapter 15
Please oh Please Can I Go?

"It's easy to believe in magic when you're young. Anything you couldn't explain was magic then. It didn't matter if it was science or a fairy tale. Electricity and elves were both infinitely mysterious and equally possible - elves probably more so."

-Charles de Lint

Maine – 2005

Jedda was blabbering a million miles a minute, and Diane couldn't make much sense of what her daughter was going on about. "Jedda. Honey? Have you even breathed in the last minute or two? Really I am trying very hard to understand, but you are babbling. Why don't you slow down a little and explain to me from the beginning."

An exaggerated sigh was the response. "Mom, I went to see the Grandmother today. She says that I'm ready." Jedda was bouncing around the living room.

"I didn't know you were going to see Grandma today. And ready? Ready for what?"

"No, not Grandma. The Grandmother!" Jedda emphasized the word as if doing so would make much of a difference in her mother's comprehension.

"Jedda, I am still not sure who you are referring to."

Jedda breathed. She supposed if she wanted to get her mother's permission for what she was about to ask she ought to slow down and explain. Something like patience was required in this particular situation.

"Okay, Mom. I am going to try to start from the beginning. You know Lou has been teaching me, right?"

It was late in the evening, Diane had just gotten home from her shift at the hospital, and really she just wanted to relax. Diane responded, clearly exhausted: "Yes, I suppose. I'm not exactly sure what it is, though, that you have been learning. You talk about meditation and energy. Okay. But is it like a school? And what is the point of it all?"

"Mom, learning and living is the point. The universe is filled with magic and mystery and I am simply seeking to understand! Remember you always used to teach me about faeries and magic and…"

"Yes, but…that was just to inspire you, to kick-start your imagination, to…"

"Mom! What are you saying? You don't believe in what you, yourself, used to tell me?"

"Honey, it's not like that. Yes, I believe to some degree in magic, but life still goes on. You can't simply live completely in these fantasy worlds. It isn't healthy."

"Mom, you don't understand. Why do I feel like you are patronizing me right now? I am trying to explain something that is really important to me. Can you please try to make an effort to be interested in something other than your job? Like my life?"

"Now who's patronizing? Jedda, you race in here, talking so rapidly I can hardly piece anything together. In fact, I haven't seen very much of you at all in the last year. You come, you go. You barely say three words to any of us here. Are you sure you are not spending too much time with that teacher of yours?"

This would have normally been when Jedda would have stormed off, completely frustrated. Why didn't Diane see that there was so much more to life than this? Couldn't she see that there was a bigger picture here? Meditation, energy, metaphysics were one thing, but even beyond that this had to do with planetary cycles and global awakening! Okay, she really could not afford to mess this up. This was an opportunity of a lifetime, and she really just wanted her mother's support. Maybe they had better start over.

"Okay, Mom. I'm sorry. You're right. You don't understand because I haven't been sharing very much lately. Honestly some of this stuff is so new that I'm not even sure how to share. I know I'm doing the right thing because I can feel it. It's like this stuff is new and yet it's not. Mostly what Lou teaches me is how to awaken my own gifts that I have within myself. And I think that is good."

Diane was beginning to soften a bit, "Yes, Jedda, I think it's good, too. I wish I had been able to help you with some of that, but the truth is I never really learned either." Diane turned her head slightly to rest her chin on her folded hand. She was pensive, nostalgic.

"Anyway, what I am trying to explain now is probably about two months' worth of stuff in five minutes. I am just so excited about this possibility. And I really hope you say yes."

"Well, if you're about to ask for permission to do something crazy like going to live off in some cave somewhere for two years to meditate and connect with the universe, then the answer is no. At least not until you're finished with high school." Diane smiled coyly. Although she was slightly joking, she didn't put anything past her precocious daughter.

Jedda returned the smile. She giggled. Then together they broke into laughter. They laughed so hard they were almost crying. Once they settled down, Jedda got serious.

"Mom. No. I'm not going off in some cave for two years. But I have been invited to go to Europe for a couple of weeks. It would be during spring break, so I wouldn't miss anything. And I would be with Lou the whole time and...," she trailed off, waiting expectantly for her mother to make some sort of favorable remark.

Diane started with a sigh, "Honey, I just don't know. I'm not sure we can afford it, and...."

Jedda interrupted, "We don't have to. The Moon Clan has some sort of foundation to support education such as this. They value this sort of learning, and based on the Grandmother's recommendation, would finance the whole trip!"

Jedda began explaining to her mother to the best of her ability who the Grandmother was. When she was finished, she said, "Mom, please let me go. Just think about it. Okay?"

"I will. I will think about it. I think this could be a good thing for you. I'm not making any promises, though. Let me think on it some more. I'll have to talk to your father, of course. I'll let you know by the end of this weekend."

Jedda jumped, "Okay! Right! I'm just relieved it isn't a straight 'No'. Okay." She started to walk away, then turned to look at her mother, "Mom, you didn't really think there was a possibility of me going off to live in a cave for two years, did you?"

Diane chuckled. "Jedda, honey. With you, I never know."

Chapter 16
A Fire Consumes All

"We who still labor by the cromlech on the shore. The grey cairn on the hill, when day sinks drowned in dew, Being weary of the world's empires, bow down to you, Master of the still stars and of the flaming door."

– W.B. Yeats

Maine – 2005

Vyn sat on a park bench watching the little kids on the swings. He enjoyed coming here. Seeing happy kids with their parents was a nice contrast to his mostly permanent experience. The park was close enough for him to walk and yet it was far enough away from home that he didn't worry about seeing anyone he knew. Sometimes he just needed to get away from the tight ship that Malin ran. A little breathing room was all he required. Malin rarely gave it to him.

Vyn had responded differently than the other boys, however. Most of them had what Vyn considered "power-fever". The moment Malin would give the boys a little taste of power, they let it go their heads. Teaching them a few tricks of manipulation was all it took. Some were easier to corrupt than others.

Vyn thought about how Malin had really worked hard to take them all to the tipping point. Time and again he'd shown them how to twist the ways of the traditional teachings ever so slightly in order to use them to one's advantage. "Getting ahead," he'd called it. Well, he wasn't sure how far ahead they all really were.

He couldn't say that he was completely unhappy, though. He was just really alone. He felt like that was the theme of his entire life – to be alone. Some things never changed. The only difference between before he met Malin and now was that now he had others to feel alone with.

On the outside he appeared to being doing fine. He had friends, if that was what you would call them. They were more like drones, or stomping buddies. They didn't really care about each other, though. What could he say? Misery loves company. He did have a nice girlfriend. They went out to movies and restaurants, hung around, and made out. That was what having a girlfriend was about, wasn't it? Social stimulation, keeping you from getting into too much trouble, and a little affection here and there when you got bored out of your mind. At least he remembered this one's name: Myra. Long black hair the color of crows' feathers, long legs to accompany it, and a fairly decent smile. Yeah, he liked her smile. Usually. Unless she was toying with him, which she did more often than he preferred. She was mostly tolerable, though. And Malin approved, which was most important. In the past, he hadn't wanted the boys to get involved with anyone outside their little circle. He allowed nothing to distract them from their work. He demanded focus and discipline. Fun could wait.

Why did they stay all those years? Who knew? They didn't. But Malin did. He knew the socially outcast were easy prey. He targeted them. He stalked them like a predator. And just at the perfectly lowest point in their life, he swooped in like a vulture that waits on death's door. That was how he had found all of them. They had that in common. They had something else in common, too. Their upbringing. All of them had been part of the same community at one point. At least their parents had been. And what's more is they all blamed their parents for their lot.

All except for Vyn. He didn't have parents, not anymore. He could barely recall their faces anymore. The only thing he saw when he thought of them was…a fire blazing violently. It consumed his mind and heart. He watched it in horror as it burned its way through everything he'd ever known. The conflagration destroyed his life. And with it most of his memories. Whenever he tried to remember anything from before – his parents, his home, growing up in California – all he saw was the flames. So he didn't. He didn't think about it. He didn't waste useless hours trying to remember what once was, but never would be again. He didn't. He couldn't. He just wouldn't go there.

After the death of his parents, he'd spent a little over a year in the foster-care system – until Malin found him. It had been right around his twelfth birthday. Malin had told him, "Everything is going to change now. We're very lucky that we've found each other." Malin spoke of him like he'd attained some sort of prize, which at first Vyn had really liked. It was different. New. Many of the foster homes had been temporary. Two months had been the longest period. Then just when he was getting used to some form of stability, he was moved again. Some were mean, while others were just indifferent. Mostly they just treated him like he was a "nobody." And he was a "nobody." With no family, no friends, nothing to call his own, how could he be anything else?

He knew that he frightened them. At first, everything would be normal. Just when everything was calm and peaceful and everyone was settling in was when the nightmares of the fire would start up again. They became more and more violent and the...no, he mustn't think of it now. Keep it out.

Malin had been the answer to his prayers. Finally someone who liked him for him. Someone who could recognize that he wasn't a "nobody." No! He was a person who mattered! At least that was what Malin told him. That was how he built him up. He didn't really need to strip him down. Not like the others. The system had already done that. The system and the...he saw the fire burning once again. Once he let it in, it would keep coming back. The images would not leave him. Peace would be elusive now.

The fire burst into insatiable flames, destroying everything in sight. Screams. He could hear his parents calling his name, "Vyncent! Vyncent!" They screamed just before the fire silenced them forever. Only now they weren't silenced.

"Vyn! Vyncent!"

Jolted from his horrific memory, he looked up, half expecting his parents to be there. These torturous memories always left him in a delirium.

"Vyn, snap out of it! It's me, Gus! What the hell are you doing anyway?" Vyn stared at the red-haired, pudgy boy that stood before him. Vyn was still confused, and only beginning to shake off the eerie hold the vision had over him.

"I thought I heard my parents. They were calling me. They were screaming my name. Just like before. Like that day that they…," he trailed off.

Even now he couldn't bring himself to utter the words. Those words seemed so final as if once he spoke them aloud then there was no changing anything. He wondered even today if he could have changed it somehow. He wondered if there were anything he could have done that would have made a difference.

"Your parents. Dude, I thought your parents were…."

Seeing the look of grief on Vyn's face, Gus thought twice before stating the obvious. He supposed he didn't need to hammer the idea home. Not today. Besides Gus's insistence on Vyn accepting what he couldn't change didn't really stem from genuine concern. His constant badgering came from a darker place, and that place was one of selfishness and jealousy. Gus knew that. And so did Vyn.

"Never mind," Gus let up, to Vyn's surprise.

Gus continued, "But come on. We have to go. Malin's pissed that you weren't at the meeting."

The meeting! Right, how could I have forgotten? Crap! He thought to himself.

"Damn. Is he really angry? I completely lost track of time," Vyn said, hoping that it wasn't as bad as he thought.

"Yeah, I figured. And I don't know. He's definitely not pleased."

Vyn sighed. He was used to messing up, just not where Malin was concerned. Ever since Malin had "rescued" him, Vyn felt this overly compensative need to please him. He needed his approval. He didn't care about anyone else, but Malin's approval was what drove him. Probably unhealthy, he knew, but it was all he had.

Vyn sighed loudly, "All right. Let's go. Time to face the music."

No one wanted to displease Malin. They didn't all have the attachment that Vyn had to the guy, but they certainly had all tested him at one time, and the outcome wasn't pretty. He was behind them until he wasn't, and if he wasn't…well, then it was all over. You didn't want to get on this guy's bad side. Not that he really had a good one. At least not that Gus could see.

Gus stuck with Malin because he was the first one to make Gus feel like he wasn't a worm on a hook, helpless and at the mercy of the cruel and cold world. He taught him about power. He made him realize that he liked power; he craved it. But all the power he'd ever known was connected to Malin. Malin kept him dangling that way. He gave him just enough to want more, and yet not enough to be self-sufficient. Malin was smart like that. Gus appreciated his shrewdness even while recognizing it was ruthless and diabolical.

"I'm sure it'll be fine. Come on," Gus lied. It wouldn't be fine. It never was. But he wasn't coming back empty-handed. He wasn't going to make that mistake today.

Chapter 17
Return to the Circle

"...it is part of the pattern of the story that has been mine to pursue – whether through the Forest of Broceliande or through the forest in my head, I leave it to others to decide."

-John Matthews, *The Song of Taliesin*

At first glance it seemed a glorious summer's day, but tiny indications pointed to something else. The marmots had grown fat, and the deer were particularly skittish. Already in formation, the birds were flying toward somewhere far away from here. The berries had mostly been picked and eaten by all the bears. All were preparing as if for a winter colder than had ever been seen before. Then the wind picked up strength, brushing through the trees as they suddenly turned their leaves into glass wind chimes clinking against one another.

And there in the Forest was a young girl. She stood softly, her eyes big and bright and filled with curiosity at what she witnessed here this day. Beauty sprawled out in the four directions, but there was something else – something underlying. Like an internal compass that pointed the way, a tone inside her heart told her she was getting closer – closer to the perfect circle, closer to the answers.

She arrived at what took on the appearance of a misted veil. What lay hidden just beyond one couldn't be sure. But the young girl was sure, and she was determined. She approached the mists and held up her hand with tender intention, as if directing an orchestra. Like a curtain drawn aside, the mists parted. There standing, tall and proud, was the perfect circle of trees, and in the center was the Great Oak himself that protruded from the ground with might and majesty.

After entering the circle, the young girl walked up steadily and calmly to the Great Oak. She knew when she had needed answers once before this was where she had found them. She drew near enough to place her delicate hands upon the Old One's massive trunk. Its girth was so large that it could have easily held within its circumference a small elephant. There were no elephants to be found, though, in the Forest. Just as the young girl was about to press her hands into the rough and scaly bark something stirred from within the tree. It blinked and flickered. The trunk swirled as if it were made of liquid. Then out from the tree stepped an amorphous being of pure luminescence. Within seconds its form began to solidify into a body made of the starlit night. Her flowing golden locks spilled over her shoulders. A long and streaming gossamer gown of pure silk draped over her form. The garment surely made of moonlight took on a greenish opalescent tint as if she and the tree were one.

The young girl recognized this being. Taken by surprise, she took a step backward and gasped.

"Elysinia..."

"Yes, Jedda Rose. I am glad you have come. It has been long, no? Are you ready to see? Are you ready to fulfill your destiny?"

"To fulfill what destiny?" This dream was all too real.

"To awaken those who slumber."

"Those who slumber," she repeated softly as if allowing time for the memory to also awaken.

"Yes, my Rose. Only you can stir his heart to remember. It is time – time for the dragons to awaken."

"The dragons?" This was all so new and yet so familiar.

"Yes. The dragons."

"I didn't even know they were real," Jedda questioned.

"Not so long ago you didn't know any of this was real," Elysinia gently reminded her.

"Yes...," Jedda was pensive. She thought about the lesson Lou had intended to teach her.

"The Great Oak showed you a tiny sliver of your vast history. It was what you needed to see then. Well, everything is going to change now because you must help us."

"Help how?" Jedda wanted to know.

"With your faery light," Elysinia said, continuing her soft and gentle tone.

"I can help to awaken the dragons with my light?"

"You cannot awaken the dragons, my Rose – but you can awaken one who can. From there the rest will be up to him."

"What do you mean?"

"Taivyn."

Jedda's heart skipped a beat. Then it started beating rapidly. "Taivyn?" After all this time even a mere mention of the boy's name affected her in such a way. She had wrestled with this feeling for almost a year. Now the Faery One was telling her that she could see him once again. Was that even possible? She looked around half believing that he might appear.

"Not here, Jedda. Not now."

"But I don't understand." Jedda was confused and sad.

"You will. Remember. Time is not what it seems. Not at all. Remember that. Go now. Awaken!"

Maine – 2005

J edda awoke in her bed drenched in perspiration. Another dream. And this one was so intense. She recalled being in the circle of trees having a conversation with…Elysinia? What were they talking about? She had the faintest image of the Great Oak and the faery woman. And Taivyn…had he been there this time?

Knock, knock, knock!

Someone was at her bedroom door. "Come in!" she yelled.

"Were you sleeping? Sorry to wake you, honey. It's so rare for you to take naps – I didn't realize you were sleeping." It was Jedda's parents.

"That's okay. I just must've dozed off." Jedda wondered what they wanted. It was unlikely that the two of them came in for a tag team, unless she was really in trouble for something. She hoped that wasn't the case.

Her mom sat down on her bed next to her, while her father remained standing in the doorway. They were uncharacteristically calm. She couldn't read them. What was going on?

"Well honey, we just wanted to come tell you. We've had a chance to talk about it, and...well, we think you should go."

It took Jedda a second to realize what they were talking about. She had just awakened. She scratched her head, "Huh?"

Then it came to her. "Mom! Dad! You're not talking about Europe are you? Oh My God! Is that what we're talking about?"

They just looked at her for a second. "Well, guys, don't keep me in suspense! Is it?"

Her mother looked at her, then at her father. Then she turned back to Jedda and smiled.

"Woohoo! Yes! Yes! Yes! I knew you would say 'yes'! I just knew it!"

Jedda started jumping up and down on her bed. Her covers fell onto the floor. She bent down and hugged her mom. Then she jumped off the bed to hug her father. She hopped around the room like a crazy person.

"Yes! Yes! Yes!" Jedda continued chanting joyfully.

"Yes, you can go. Just don't hitchhike, okay?" her father eyed her.

"Of course I won't hitchhike! Dad!"

"Yes, and you'll have to call at least once while you're gone so we know you're all right, okay?"

"Yes, Mom. Of course!"

Her father gave her another hug and left the room. Her mother hugged her and walked to the door. Before she left she turned to Jedda.

"Oh, and honey, go find some of that magic we used to talk about."

Chapter 18
For Your Journey

"What we see and what we imagine have one connected life, but it is only when we enter into dialogue with the otherworld that we understand this."

– Caitlin Matthews, *Celtic Visions*

The Forest – 11,000 BCE (3 months after GG)

Taivyn didn't know how to deal with what had happened. Why had she done it? Amelda had spoken as if she could have done something to prevent it. He dug forcefully. Filled with anger and sadness, the same questions continued to spin around in his head like a revolving door of night terrors: *Why did she have to leave? Why did she do this?* He was so tired. He had been so happy here with her. For the first time in his life, safety and comfort had felt real. He shoveled the ground over her lifeless body. He didn't want to just leave her there. He'd never buried someone before, and didn't even know if he was doing it correctly. Normally they burned the bodies afloat on a funeral pyre, but the only water around was that blasted well.

He finished interring the old woman who he'd loved like a grandmother. They'd taken care of each other over the past few months. Except for the Forest creatures, he was alone again.

He poured the last pile of dirt onto the grave. As he picked the red and orange fire blossoms, hot tears ran down his face. The fire blossom had been her favorite flower, and so he placed as many of them as he could find on top of the burial site. The family of black squirrels she used to feed scurried at his feet. They would miss more than just the bread she fed them. Hovering on a branch near to him, a black bird, most probably a raven, cawed loudly. Taivyn had never noticed him before, but then again he hadn't paid much attention to the animals as of late. A tiny yellow pointed hat revealed a gnome attempting concealment at the base of a large hawthorn tree. Amelda had been loved by so many in the Forest. The dreams had kept him so occupied he had never really noticed to what extent.

Kneeling down, Taivyn closed his eyes in prayer. He prayed to the Mother of All to take Amelda back into her womb. He sent love and blessings into the Earth to support Amelda's soul on its journey to the next world. Tears continued to pour from his eyes.

Why had she left him? Everyone left. Everyone. He used a few stones to mark where she was interred. Someone should know she was here. Even if no one ever did. She should be remembered for her warmth, her kindness!

Chapter 19
A Mushroom Never Meanders

*"I believe in God...who reveals Himself in the
orderly harmony of the universe. I believe that
Intelligence is manifested throughout all Nature.
The basis of scientific work is the conviction
that the world is an ordered and comprehensible
entity and not a thing of chance."*

– Albert Einstein[1]

The Forest – 11,000 BCE (3 months after GG)

The one who followed behind was careful, knowing far too well the consequence of even blinking an eye. He couldn't lose track of the being that he tailed so closely. Crystal in hand, he continued to record the movements that he witnessed, as well as those that he

---

[1] *Quoted from The Essential Unity of all Religions (pp. 22, 23, & 24), by Bhagavan Das, M.A., D. Litt., Benares and Allahabad Universities.*

didn't. More and more however, the crystal was increasingly unwilling to participate in its duty.

The Dark One was hot in pursuit turning this way and that. He didn't care about the small beings he trod underfoot in his thoughtlessness. Nor did he bother about the plants that he crushed in his path. He was a wretched excuse for a human being, so marred by his distorted sense of self-righteousness, he had all but lost his humanity. He raged through the Forest, his dark thoughts a pollution that made the birds wince and gasp for air. How had one born of the light turned in such a way?

The Dark One was desperate and determined in his hunt. He did not need to capture the small being that gave him chase. That would have been easy enough. No, he just needed to stalk it, observing and recording its moves, so that when the time came he would be ready. He would have the key to this great power soon enough. And then he would have what it was he truly desired. The dragons!

He picked up his pace, not wanting to fail in his mission. He plowed through a small bush, trampling it to the ground. He swooped over a low hanging branch, and waited. Where had the being gone? He had just seen it underneath the leaves here. Now it had suddenly disappeared. Drat!

A shrill groan not unlike the sound of death and something darker was heard throughout the Forest near and far. The mark was lost to him…for now.

Chapter 20
Hello Mother...

"We have so much to give humans, if they would only relax in us, and great healing power is ours for you to turn to. We are guardians of the earth in many ways and humans should be part of what we guard."

- A Scots Pine in Dorothy Maclean, *Call of the Trees*

Maine – 2005

As far as anyone knew, she was the oldest and wisest member of the Moon Clan that lived today. Those seeking advice on matters big and small valued her age-old wisdom. It was this reason, and this reason alone, that had earned her the title of the Grandmother. In fact, she didn't have any grandchildren. At least not by blood. In truth, she thought of many as her grandchildren. Like a flock, she helped to guide them until they could hear the voice within their own hearts strong and true.

She thought of Lou. How proud of her she was. Of course, some might argue she was a bit biased, for she alone had instructed her since she was a young girl. Now Lou was a woman with her own students to teach. And boy, did she have her hands full with that one. Jedda. *Sharp one, that one*, she thought to herself. A little impetuous maybe, but that was true of almost all teenagers these days. After all, these days there was really only one requirement for embarking on this path as far as the Grandmother was concerned. And that was love. One had to be pure in their intentions to pursue this way of life.

In this department the young girl checked out. She could feel it when sitting with her. It was really the only reason she had requested the visit. She wanted to see for herself. Not that she didn't trust Lou. She trusted her wholeheartedly. She knew Lou would find her. After all, Great Spirit would never fail. Mankind could fail in its efforts, but not the divine. She had faith. As long as there still existed those who walked with an earnest desire to awaken their hearts, there would be an opportunity upon this planet for humankind.

The Grandmother's time on the Earth plane was coming to a close. All plans had been set into motion as best as they could be. Now it would be up to each one to play their respective roles. It would take many working together, and not just those of the human variety. It would require discipline and commitment. Most of all, it would require heart, pure love and devotion for the highest good of all concerned.

Yes, love was the only requirement. A sigh rose from the Grandmother's lips. Her thoughts glided nostalgically to the past. Sadness drizzled like tiny drops of rain across her memories. She reminded herself that she had done all she could back then. Still her human nature took over and she racked her brain, wondering if there might have been some solution to what obviously had gone awry. When had it gone awry, though? She didn't believe in pure evil. Nor did she buy into the idea of having a predisposition to doing bad things. Of course, she knew that there was a Higher Law at work, a law which sometimes even eluded her. She breathed deeply in an effort to release *him* once and for all to Great Spirit's care.

The streaming pink rays of the setting sun still trickled through the soft curtains, casting a rich glow on the Persian rug that warmed her feet. She smiled, comforted by the delicate heat, but also by something more.

The Grandmother knew Lou had been well-prepared for this. Since childhood the foundation had been laid. She had also known all along Lou would find the girl, for she had "seen" it many years ago. Lou would now do all she could in order to ensure Jedda received the proper training. After all, besides being a Keeper, Lou was also the Grandmother's niece.

The Grandmother was rocking in her chair contentedly when the phone rang. She rose to answer it. She walked over to the small end table where the phone sat in its cradle.

"Hello?"

The person on the other line waited a moment before speaking. A sick feeling ran through the old woman that made her blood go cold. Then a raspy voice on the other line finally hissed, "Hello, mother…."

Chapter 21
Across the Big Pond

"Faeries are seen not by the eyes but through the heart."

-Brian Froud, *Good Faeries, Bad Faeries*

England – 2005

Next stop, England, in a small and scarcely populated village. Green hedges lined the countryside. A long plane ride, an hour by train, and a bus ride later found Lou and Jedda alighting in Amesbury. Sprinkled with small farms and cottages, the village was charming and quaint.

Lou had some friends who had invited them to be their guests for the day and stay the night. They arrived around one o'clock in the afternoon on Saturday. The house was a beautiful Victorian estate on an old farm. The farm was no longer in use, but the grounds were quite marvelous. The hedgerows were magical and made of hawthorns. There was a perfect English cottage garden that greeted all who entered the property; it was filled with wild herbs, flowers and tall grasses.

The Hatters were a lovely couple and Jedda liked them almost immediately. The woman was tall and dark-haired. She wore her long hair with a tiny braid on either side that was brought back away from her face and pinned in a bun. The rest of her hair fell down her back. With soft wrinkles just forming on the corners of her eyes – mostly from smiling probably, which she seemed to do a lot of –, she appeared to be in her early fifties.

Just slightly taller than the woman, the man had a slim but fit build. His black hair was starting to fill in with silvery grey strands that suited his coffee-colored complexion quite well. On his face, he usually wore glasses, but would occasionally remove them, which made him look a bit more relaxed.

"Hello Lou! It is so good to see you. Ah! It's been ages!" The dark haired woman spoke emphatically.

"Katerina, it's been too long. But my, you haven't changed! You look marvelous! And Joe, how are you! How happy I am to be here with you, my friends!"

"Yes, well, we are certainly glad that you gave us a ring. What good fortune we were in town! And who might this lovely young lady be?" Joe asked, looking at Jedda.

"Katerina, Joe, may I present to you, my friend and student, Jedda."

"Jedda! What a lovely name! We are delighted to meet you! Tell us, is this your first time to England?"

"Yes it is, actually. I am really excited to be here and I am very pleased to meet you."

"Ah look at that! The girl has such wonderful manners! What a fine American you are, Love! Do come in and make yourselves comfortable. We were just preparing some sandwiches and tea. Would you like to lunch with us in the drawing room?" Joe's warm invitation was music to their tired feet.

"We'd love to. We're famished. Thank you very much!" said Lou, speaking for them both.

They walked through the large hall that led into the drawing room. After admiring the large Turkish tapestries on the wall, Jedda made herself comfortable in one of the richly upholstered chairs. Lou sat next to her on the other, while the couple relaxed on the sofa. They spent lunch in comfortable conversation. After finishing their refreshment they suggested that Jedda and Lou rest a bit before dinner. They assured them they would have plenty of time for lively discussion later that evening.

"Would it be all right if I just took a walk? I am tired, but I don't think my excitement will allow me to sleep," Jedda asked with a glowing enthusiasm.

Joe mused, "Ah, to be young again…."

The adults chuckled, not surprised by the young girl's spirit. Katerina, noticing Jedda's eagerness to get some fresh air, answered, "Of course, Jedda. The grounds are quite lovely."

"Enjoy yourself, Jedda. There is magic in this countryside," Lou said just before looking up toward the grand staircase that led up to the guest rooms.

Joe, catching the hint, led Lou up to her room so she could rest before dinner. Almost like a ballerina, Katerina waived to Jedda, her arm extending out gracefully and powerfully.

"Come, Jedda. The back door is this way, and from there I can point out to you a nice path to take. Unless you'd like me to go with you…?"

Jedda didn't have to answer. She knew from the look in her eye that the girl wished to enjoy some solitude. Katerina smiled.

"Don't worry. I didn't think you wanted company. I only wanted to make sure. We can't have you returning to the States and saying your hosts had no manners." Katerina laughed, and her thick hair shook slightly.

"I would never," Jedda assured her.

This made Katerina laugh even more. They walked over to two large French doors with glass panes. The double doors opened out to an expansive pastoral setting that stretched for miles ahead. The only containment came from the trees and hedges that dotted the right and left edges of the land. Katerina pointed through the glass, almost directly ahead of them.

"There," Katerina said, "just in the distance is a little path. You can't see it from here, but it starts just on the other side of that footbridge over there."

Jedda could easily make out the footbridge that crossed over a small pond. Tall, verdant grasses could be seen peeking out of the water where a large blue heron stood, searching for fish to eat. The heron large, and its body looked strong and delicate at the same time. The bird reminded Jedda of Katerina for some reason.

As if reading her thoughts, Katerina commented, "Ah, the blue heron. She is a favorite of mine. If she graces us with her presence at all, it is always around this time of day. A good omen for your walk, I suspect." Katerina had a glimmer in her eye.

"I didn't know blue heron were found in the UK," said Jedda, a hint of wonder in her voice.

"We didn't either. Until we saw this one. She began showing up several years ago. Things are changing…," Katerina mused as she trailed off. Bringing herself back from her dreamlike state, she continued, "So take the path just after the bridge. It will curve ever so slightly to the left. You will come to a crossroads after five minutes or so. Take the path to the left. The other two lead to open fields, which are nice, but I think you will enjoy the left path the most."

"Where does the path to the left lead?" Jedda asked. Her curiosity had gotten the best of her.

"It leads where many paths in the English countryside lead – to hidden doorways and enchanting places." Katerina winked at Jedda. It seemed that was the only preamble Jedda was going to get. That was just fine. Jedda loved the mystery with which Katerina had infused the situation.

Katerina offered Jedda a fuzzy wrap, which would prevent her from having to dig through her suitcase. "Just in case the winds pick up. You won't have to turn back prematurely, or worst endure the chill while pressing on."

Katerina must have sensed Jedda's aversion to cold weather. The sun had made an appearance, but mostly it still struggled with the cumulus clouds for the stage. The silver outline of the whitish grey puffy masses suggested that it had not yet given up. However, one could never rely on British weather not to take a turn for the worst. Contrary to popular belief, Jedda thought the weather gave England its charm. A surreal effect, like that created by twilight and midsummer, seemed to pervade the grey skies. And it reminded Jedda of home.

Maine is not unlike this. Perhaps England is my home away from home.

Showing Jedda outside the glass doors, Katerina led the young girl almost halfway to the bridge. "Do you think you have it from here?"

Jedda nodded. She had no fear of getting lost. Maybe she would have been afraid in a big city, but in the woods and countryside Jedda was at home.

"Have a lovely walk, Love. Keep your eyes peeled. There are all sorts of magical creatures in these parts." Katerina winked again. Jedda looked over at the heron that still stood its ground in the pond. The bird had stopped looking for fish, and was now watching the two ladies intently. *What a majestic creature,* Jedda thought. If the heron was any indication to the array of fauna in this area, then Jedda couldn't wait to see what surprises awaited her.

Chapter 22
Magical Things in the Hedgerow

*"Growing up is nothing more
than aging without growing."*

-Ted Andrews, *Enchantment of the Faerie Realm*

England – 2005

Jedda made her way to the small pond and crossed the footbridge. She turned to wave to Katerina, assuring her new friend that she could handle it from hcre. The dark-haired woman waved back, and returned to the house. Jedda watched the woman disappear inside.

Jedda made her way along the path until she arrived at the crossroads of which Katerina had informed her. Without thinking about it, she naturally took the recommended path that curved to the far left. The walk was indeed lovely, the borders of the path sprinkled with Queen Anne's lace and ground ivy. Apple trees formed a natural arbor ahead, their thin bark easily allowing for inosculation. Jedda walked under the interwoven canopy of trees. Almost to the other end of the tree tunnel, she noted a soft smoky mist had descended creating a fuzzy view of what lay in the distance.

It was during this time that her focus was drawn to a strange feeling that someone or something was watching her. It wasn't an eerie sensation at all, however. Instead of being worried, Jedda felt exhilarated and began lightly skipping. She exited the tunnel, and just as soon as it had arisen, the mist dissipated as if it were never there.

Now the footpath was bordered on either side by artfully pleached hawthorns. The branches of these trees did not extend overhead as the apple trees' branches had, but instead grew into neatly manicured hedgerows. Captivated by their intricacy, Jedda walked closely to the hedges. Two flashing twinkles stopped her in her tracks. She knelt to inspect the place in the hedges where she had spotted the light. Admiring the interwoven world that had been created, she peered deeply inside the trees' branches. It was impossible to tell which branches belonged to which trees, so complexly were they intertwined with one another.

Her eyes studied the area, carefully watching for any movement. There, deep within the hedges, could be discerned a gleaming light. Certain that the sun had not come out to play Jedda stared at the luminescent ray, knowing that what she witnessed before her was something otherworldly. As if highlighting that which was previously hidden, the ray flickered and a roundish doorway appeared. What she thought to be gnomes and pixies guarded the opening. Instead of feeling dissuaded to approach, a gentle song of flower petals and flutes danced through the air, stirring the girl's heart. The smallish otherworldly creatures enticed her lovingly to enter. Accustomed to tree portals, Jedda thoughtlessly slipped through a gap that had not hitherto been there.

****

Jedda stared out from the underbrush. She was so closely pressed up against the scratchy branches, she could barely see the leaves that hung low on the trees just above her. The light reflected off the leaves in a way that told her she was not in England any longer. Like little jewel boxes all lit up and twirling around, the leaves glimmered even when the source of light could not be determined.

Leaves never looked like that in my world. She gasped. *The Forest!*

Jedda squeezed between the branches, careful not to scrape herself on the thorns. As far as the eye could see into the distance were craggy moss-covered boulders. She had never been to this part of the Forest before.

A sudden rustling and jostling movement caught her eye. At the base of a large rock, a small and oddly balanced creature hobbled around. His head was topped with a pointy red hat. He bent over, and soon his hat, along with the rest of him, disappeared into a hole in the boulder. Jedda could hear him fumbling and digging about rather hurriedly, as he moved things to this side and that. Items started flying out from the hole, as the gnome quickly dismissed and discarded things one by one. He seemed to be hastily searching for something. A small pile was accumulating near the trees next to Jedda, as the tossed items landed somehow neatly beside her.

"Where is it?" He cried and howled. He was rummaging profusely. At last he came to a sudden halt and stared. He reached further inside the boulder. He retracted his small arm, and climbed out of the hole. Then slowly he opened his hand to reveal a beautiful red jewel.

"At last I've found you! Oh, by the Seven Seas and Two Swans! I've found it! All is not lost. I will find you, my brothers and sisters. I will. If it is the last thing I do. I swear it!"

****

Jedda rubbed her eyes. She saw the hedgerow before her. *I'm back.* She wondered who the gnome was. *Was that a ruby he was holding?* It was strange that her visit had been so fleeting. Then again it was probably for the best. Jedda looked up at the sky. It was getting dark. Soon it would be too dark to see the footpath. Not having brought a flashlight, she decided she had better start making her way back. Besides it would be time for dinner, and she didn't want to keep her hosts or Lou waiting. That would be rude. She made her way back along the hedge-lined pathway and through the tunnel. Finally she glimpsed the footbridge a few yards ahead.

When she entered the house Joe was waiting for her with a hot cup of tea. He must have seen her coming over the footbridge. He smiled earnestly. Joe reminded her of a teddy bear she once had, his manner was so warm.

"Here," he said, handing her the tea. "It's getting a bit brisk out there. This is sure to warm you up."

Jedda took the steaming beverage grateful for his intuition. Joe continued, "The ladies will be down soon. They're just getting done up for dinner. You know how you women are," Joe smiled again. "You're welcome to relax down here for a bit until the food is ready, or I can show you to your room."

"I think I'd like to freshen up a bit, if that's okay," said Jedda. She was quiet. Joe could tell she was contemplating something.

"Of course, my dear. That's no problem at all. Follow me," said Joe.

As they climbed the staircase, Joe asked, "So how was your walk? Not too cold I hope?"

"No, Katerina gave me this," Jedda said, indicating the fuzzy wrap. Then she added, "My walk was lovely and…," she paused. Jedda was unsure of how much she should share with this couple she had just met. She had been very careful not to mention much of anything to anyone besides Lou.

They arrived at the guest room that had been made up for Jedda. Joe gave the door a little nudge and it swung open.

Joe said, "Everything you need should be in there. You have your own bathroom. I've brought your luggage and set it down just over there. Do make yourself at home."

He gestured for Jedda to go inside. Before he turned to leave he added, "Oh and Jedda...there are magical things in the hedgerow, hmmm?" His eyes sparkled. Before Jedda could say anything Joe had disappeared from the doorway.

Chapter 23
An Old Moon Tale

"The language we use when we attempt to talk about spirit is of necessity highly symbolic."

- Moyra Caldecott, *Myths of the Sacred Tree*

England – 2005

Dinner was served around 7p.m. Platters of delectable dishes lined the table. There was roast duck with pomegranate and wine sauce. A wonderful array of potatoes, spinach, and wild-foraged mushrooms filled several bowls. Joe opened an exquisite vintage of wine to toast the occasion. *Boy, do these people know how to treat guests or what?*, Jedda thought to herself. She felt like a queen. They passed the dishes to one another. When all their plates were filled they blessed the food. Thus began the feast to honor their friends – one new and one old.

"So, Lou, you know we are dying to hear what brought you to the UK on such short notice. We didn't have much time to chat last week when we spoke. We do so hope you are willing to spill the beans," Katerina jested.

"Yes, well. It's a bit of a long story, but shouldn't be too much of a jump for you." Then Lou turned to Jedda, "Jedda, I didn't have a chance to tell you, but Katerina and Joe aren't just old friends, they are Moon Clan as well."

Jedda's eyes got big. That would explain the mysterious comments Katerina and Joe had made throughout the day. Jedda hadn't met anyone else from the Moon Clan other than Lou and the Grandmother – at least none of which she was aware. She had begun to wonder if any other members of the organization still existed. Now it was like she was finally meeting the "family!"

Joe and Katerina looked curiously from Lou to Jedda. Clearly they knew Jedda was not Moon Clan. While they were happy to inspire a little imagination as they had earlier with their mysterious comments, they had no intention to willingly divulge anything about the ancient organization of which they were a part. So why was Lou being so open with Jedda? The Moon Clan wasn't secretive, but definitely kept to themselves. They decided long ago that it was too dangerous to share openly with outsiders. Hell, they didn't share too openly with "insiders" these days either.

They did trust Lou's judgment, however. She was, after all, the current Keeper. The Grandmother had long since turned over the full responsibility of the position to her niece. Lou was more trustworthy than anyone they knew. Never reckless, nor naïve, Lou was a fine example for which others of the Moon Clan might strive. Lou had never failed in any endeavor she pursued, except maybe one. Then again, she had not really failed in finding a Keeper, she just had not found one yet. Perhaps there was not one to be found, they had finally wondered.

Needless to say, their curiosity was definitely piqued. What could be the Keeper's reasoning for revealing the organization to the young girl?

This is going to be interesting, Katerina thought. Her smile was almost mischievous, coaxing even.

Joe's expression was more difficult to read in the moment. A patient man who never hurried anything, especially not an explanation, he was quietly waiting for the answers to unfold.

To lighten the tension in the atmosphere, they all began eating again. This would allow Lou to explain without making everyone feel like they were on pins and needles.

Lou took the cue and finally added, "It's okay. Jedda is one of us now. And I suppose I should just go ahead and mention she's being trained to be the next Keeper!"

Joe and Katerina paused mid-bite. Shocked would have been an understatement in describing their expressions. This was unprecedented – at least as far back as anyone knew.

Without keeping them in suspense too much longer Lou began telling the tale. Joe and Katerina hardly ate a bite during the story. They couldn't believe someone outside of the Moon Clan would qualify for Keeper.

Then again, times were changing. Old ways of doing things were being reconceived anew.

Furthermore, according to Lou, the Grandmother approved of it. Well, if Lou and the Grandmother were in support of this, so were they. In the end, they were very happy and excited about the news. After all, many had been wondering if the next Keeper would ever be identified. Katerina and Joe had often spent nights in discussion on that very subject.

Lou explained a lot – but she did not tell all. She left out the part about what they were going to be doing over the next few days in a small village just to the west of Amesbury. Some things were too delicate to be discussed out loud. However, that didn't seem to stop Katerina from inquiring:

"Perhaps Jedda will be the one to lift the curse...?" Katerina blurted. Joe looked at his wife, clearly as surprised as Lou that she mentioned it. *So do they know the ancient prophecy*, Lou thought to herself.

"Curse?" Jedda asked, a little nervous.

"Well, now. I wouldn't call it a curse, Katerina. That sounds so hocus pocus, you know. No, not a curse," Lou assured.

Then she turned to Jedda: "The less you know, the better, dear. Don't worry. I would never place you in harm's way. Besides it's more or less just an old wives' tale, or in this case, an Old Moon Tale." They all laughed. The subject was left alone after that. Enjoying their company into the late evening, they talked until they could talk no more. Then it was off to bed. The adventure had only just begun.

Chapter 24
In Darkness We Prepare

"The iron tongue of midnight hath told twelve;
lovers to bed; 'tis almost fairy time."

– William Shakespeare, *A Midsummer Night's Dream*

The Forest – 11,000 BCE (4 months after GG)

They were camped strategically on the outskirts of the Forest. Stragglers and outcasts, many of them had been ostracized from their villages or communities for one dark reason or another. They had strategized long and hard, for they intended to harness the opportunity of the darkness that brewed. Those pesky Keepers weren't the only ones with tricks up their sleeves. Now the Dark One had devised a way to manipulate power in order to control the ages!

The dragons were the answer to their plan. Of course this was a very delicate matter because one did not simply call forth the dragons on a whim. No, that would be suicide, for the dragons did not respond well to manipulation. Regardless of all the stories that might have been told, the dragons were a noble race of beings and only worked with those pure of heart. That is why they took such a great risk to steal the crystal – a very special crystal indeed.

They stared at its egg-shaped and luminescent surface. Gazing into its depths, only swirling light and mist could be seen, obscuring what lay beyond. It glowed gold and then blue from time to time. Stored within it was information encoded in the Language of Light – Elyrie – and so it could not be read by just anyone. It was a good thing that the confounded gnome had finally cooperated when he did.

Named for the ancient dragon prophecy that it held, this crystal was known as the Prophecy Egg. Contained within it was not just a prophecy, however. For it also contained something else: the light codes essential for identifying the members of the Dragon Clan.

The Prophecy Egg changed shades from light to dark and back again. It was now in the hands of those who wished to use its contents for selfish gain. Now as everyone knows, crystals are not inanimate rocks; they are conscious beings of light. Their consciousness is different from what humans think of as being alive, however they grow and they can feel. This crystal knew that it must get away, for it could feel the fear building in the atoms around it. The Prophecy Egg needed to awaken!

One of the elders stood. Animal skins worn around his shoulders demonstrated his power over nature. His voice was gruff and his skin was weatherworn. He glared at the group, and the dance of rage was reflected in his eyes. The effects of unchecked power had taken their toll, and all could see he had been completely consumed. None dared to cross him. This one had been the first to fall to the darkness that came upon them. He did not wish to glide through the Age of Sleep – he had another plan in mind. While all slept throughout the age, he would seize control.

When first obtained, the Prophecy Egg appeared opaque, still indicating that not a single member of the notorious clan existed. Surely then the beasts would have to respond to him. The Dark One had hoped that the power from the Crossing of the Frog and the Mushroom coupled with the energy signature of the Prophecy Egg would be exactly what he required. Unless there were one who still lived. That could thwart his plan entirely.

There had been no indications, however, that any of *them* remained. Long ago had his aunt drunk of the waters that made her unable to dream with the dragons. For what reason she had done this he knew not! He only knew she had, for her aging skin had told him so. His uncle had died shortly after from heartache. A soft-hearted fool he was! They both were! They had been the last.

The Dark One had hunted high and low just to be sure. He had found nothing. Then a less than year ago, something changed. He had had the Prophecy Egg in his possession for several months when an indication of life swirled within the crystal's surface! One still lived.

But who? He had searched the Forest thoroughly and nothing had turned up.

Then one night he was on his way to the Moon Clan. Visiting the community sporadically kept him off their radar. He led them to believe that he was fulfilling his tasked role dutifully. For almost a decade he had been tasked to track the movements of the mysterious creature known as the mushroom. At first he had grumbled over it. However, he had quickly changed his tune when he realized the opportunity that lay before him. After tracking the being for over a year, the Dark One noticed that the mushroom started to exhibit the signs – signs that it was getting ready to cross paths with the frog. Of course, 'getting ready' could mean a fairly long time, as time was always relative. So the Dark One had continued to track the being and bide his time. To anyone at the Moon Clan it had appeared that he was doing as he was bidden. But the truth was he had tired of their Earth-loving ways long ago.

Good-natured and weak! That is what that blasted community is!

The last time he had gone to visit the Moon Clan was the night that everything had changed. It was four months ago, and he had nearly arrived at his wretched destination, probably only four or five miles away. Suddenly, he had felt something move in the darkness. It moved too clumsily to be an animal unless it were an ailing creature. He smiled. He liked the thought of helpless creatures ailing. Then the treasure that he carried with him started vibrating in the folds of his clothes. Removing the Prophecy Egg from its hiding place, he examined it closely. Sure enough, the swirling light had become more pronounced until it concentrated into one single point.

So it is true! One still lives! My revenge may be more satisfying than I ever suspected! Then he saw the boy. Like a bumbling fool, the boy stumbled through the Forest. *How can it be! An ingrate such as he should take what is rightfully mine! Curse them all!* He knew exactly who the boy was. That which he had sought had been hidden in plain sight all these years. He shuddered to think what might have happened if that loose end should be left untied. The boy could be his undoing!

He followed the boy closely. Unfortunately, the idiot had sensed his presence and had bolted. The Dark One gave chase and was soon tailing him, but it was no use. He had lost him after a time. When he had finally picked up his trail again, it was too late. The boy sat crouched near an oddly familiar enclosure of trees. A fire could be seen blazing. Who could be in these parts at this hour? Only humans used campfires. The Dark One inched closer, not wanting to give himself away again. Then he spied them – Master Ra-Ma'at and the pesky gnome. *Drat!* He could not risk the gnome squealing. The Dark One knew that it was fear that kept the gnome from spilling the beans. The gnome could not lie, though. If the Dark One were to show himself, the gnome's reaction would surely give him away.

Satisfied with his discovery, the Dark One retreated. He did not continue his journey to the Moon Clan, though. Instead he went back to his camp where others of like-mind had started to gather. Supporters, he called them. Yes, it was in this camp that he had been able to further develop his scheme.

His wheels had started to turn. At first he had thought to kill the boy. He would just do away with the problem. Then a twisted smile crept across his already contorted face. *In fact, this could be the missing part of my nearly foolproof formula.* The Crossing of the Frog and the Mushroom could possibly give him what he needed, but what if the dragons still didn't respond. How infuriating he found their unwillingness to recognize his authority! No, he would not leave anything to chance. To ensure the success of his plan, he would require something more....

He stood there with the blaze raging before him. The fire made the madness within him appear amplified. Finally, he spoke, "It is time we take what is ours. The Crossing of the Frog and the Mushroom is nearly upon us. It is time now we find Taivyn Green."

Chapter 25
Friends Among Us

"...the 'Medicine Wheel Garden,'...a multidimensional garden where we become co-creators with nature and magic happens."

-Thea Summer Deer, *Wisdom of the Plant Devas*

England – 2005

The plan was to arrive in Somerset by late morning Sunday. They'd spend the day settling in – a little walking around, maybe some shopping. Monday would be the big day – the Tor of Avalantia. About an hour into the bus trip, Jedda and Lou were wondering if they had missed their stop. The bus was crowded and so making their way to the driver was not going to be easy. Jedda stood up and looked out. Why couldn't they just call out the names of the stops? That would make things so much easier. They were beginning to fret when something quite unexpected happened.

"Good day, to you both. Where might you be headed on this fine morning?"

A little old lady with white hair had addressed them. Old is probably an understatement. Ancient might be better suited on this occasion. She wore a light blue duster that really made her eyes stand out – like two large and perfectly cut pieces of azurite. She smiled and that made them sparkle like the stars in the heavens. Quite petite in stature, she couldn't have been much taller than Jedda. Perhaps she was slightly taller, because no one was that short.

Jedda and Lou both smiled at her. Lou answered, "We're headed to Avalantia, but it seems we may have missed it. We're not quite used to the buses here."

"Well, today must be your lucky day. For starters, you haven't missed it."

"We haven't? Oh by the Grace of Great Spirit. Thank goodness." Lou and Jedda both looked relieved.

"In fact, that's my stop as well!" The old woman seemed as enthusiastic as they were.

"Really?" Jedda was excited now. And typical of every teenager: "How much farther is it?"

"Well, you see how the road begins to climb in the distance just ahead?" They shook their heads in the affirmative. "Well, we'll go up and over. Just as we start to make our way down into the valley we'll be coming into the village of Avalantia." The ancient woman smiled.

"Keep your eyes peeled when we start to descend," the woman continued, "just to the left we'll catch a glimpse of the Tor."

"The Tor?" Jedda's eyes were wide with anticipation.

"Yes, it's an old English word for hill. This one is the Tor of Avalantia. Even to this very day every time I see it, it's like seeing it for the first time. An eerie feeling still comes over me."

"Eerie?" Jedda didn't like the sound of that.

"Well, yes. You know. Strange. Supernatural is probably a better word, I suspect." The old woman smiled.

The bus began its ascent. Making its way to the top was slow going. Face glued to the window, Jedda wasn't going to miss a thing. They reached the highest point. The clouds were a wash of pink and yellow haze. A ray of sunlight peeked out and stretched its way through the valley like a string of gold that lit the way. Now they began their descent.

There in their midst rose a thing of surreal beauty. The sun streaming through the clouds seemed to point right to it. Crowned by a lone tower, the hill cast a shadow on the lands below. The clouds moved like puffs of smoke and it was as if Jedda could feel them moving within her. Mesmerized by that hill in the distance, she couldn't take her eyes off it. Like a magnet it pulled on her heart and soul, beckoning her as if it were home. She watched intensely as the dance the sun did with the clouds created a marvelous light show of colors that changed around it. Then on the side of the hill and just for a moment a doorway fluttered into sight. Jedda blinked and rubbed her eyes.

"May I present the Tor of Avalantia." The initial traces of superstition in the old woman's voice had all but disappeared leaving in their place a sense of pride. It was, after all, the symbol of her village.

They alighted from the bus on Market Street, the main throughway here in town. The village was tiny, yet bustling with life.

"Do feel free to stop in for a cup of tea sometime during your stay here," said the old lady, "my little flat is just there." She pointed down the little street. "The number is 107. Do come by."

Still pondering deeply the experience, Jedda was practically mute. Lou thanked the woman and said that they would definitely consider it. The inn at which they had booked their room was just up the road and to the right. The large red sign read The Hawthorne. Jedda still hadn't spoken.

"What a blessing! Great Spirit sent us an angel to guide our way," Lou commented excitedly. Jedda just nodded.

"Dear, are you okay? You haven't said two words since we got off the bus."

"Oh yes. It's just that…I saw it again."

"Saw what?"

"The doorway. It's like a chamber. Below the hill. Below the Tor, I mean."

"Oh, I see." Lou was thoughtful, "Jedda, listen to me. I am not sharing what the legends say because I don't want that to influence your impressions. I want you to have your own experience. You are completely safe. You don't have to worry about that. And well…this is exciting!"

Jedda felt excited, too, but she also felt something else – something ancient. She kept it to herself. A tall man with reddish hair came to greet them. Jedda turned to see if she could catch one more glimpse of that entrancing hill before entering. It was no use, though – from their position in the town it was not visible. Disappointed, she stepped inside The Hawthorne and closed the door behind her.

Chapter 26
Something Lies Beneath

"Only the one who fully comprehends the difficulties of awakening can understand that long and arduous work is needed to wake up."

- G. I. Gurdjieff

England – 2005

They weren't wasting any time, so bright and early the next day they started for the Tor. The hill sat just outside of town. Through hawthorn trees and hedges, clearly marked footpaths led visitors easily enough to its base. Looming on the otherworldly hill a single tower stood as a warning to all those who might come.

"St. Michael's Tower," said Lou as if in answer to Jedda's unspoken question. "It is all that remains of the church that once stood there. The church was built in an effort to suppress the sacred teachings of the native people, which is what the hill represented."

Yet somehow the tower and the hill seemed to get along now as if they had actually grown close in all these years.

A large fence, at least a mile in circumference, encircled the area around the Tor, and a single wooden gate stood between the outside world and the final part of the footpath that led up the hill. Lou opened the gate and Jedda walked through. She was greeted with a strange visceral sensation that started in her gut and moved up to her heart. She could feel the hill's presence as they climbed, following the terracing, like an ancient spiral labyrinth that wound its way around the hillside. With every step she felt both pulled and repelled. Something invited her closer, and something told her to stay away.

Arriving on top after making their way through what seemed like an endless maze, Jedda stood in awe and wonder. Lou walked to the hill's edge. The view was stunning. Lou looked at Jedda. Her intuition told her to just let the girl be. She stepped over to a patch of grass near the tower's base and hung back.

Being able to see for miles around, Jedda spun several times, allowing the biting wind to chill her nose. Feeling invigorated, she stared at the tower that seemed to challenge her. Unwilling to let it threaten her further, she approached the archway and stepped into it. It only took about ten steps to make it to the other side. With a confident gait, Jedda trod through the small passageway. Exiting out the other archway, she found herself standing on top at the opposite side of the hill. She looked around. A sharp pull tugged at her center, and Jedda's heart began to race. As if entranced, she turned back around and gazed at the tower's passageway. Closing her eyes, she relaxed somewhat. When she opened them again, she gasped. The passageway that led to the other side had vanished, and in its place was a stairwell that descended out of sight. Her heart was now set aflame, as some familiar voice within her cried out. Without deciding to, she found herself descending the secret staircase. Down, down, down she went – whether to heaven or hell, she did not know. It felt like both, the way her stomach twisted and her skin twitched.

As if lit by flowers, the stairwell was alive with tiny life forms. Tiny elemental beings swirled and glided. However beautiful they were, an inexplicable sadness pervaded the cave-like atmosphere. Jedda descended into darkness, and yet she could see. Like a tiny torch, a soft light flickered and glowed within her chest. "She carries the green light," she heard whispered voices say.

An abrupt end in the stairs announced her arrival at the bottom where a large knot of matter hung low and dull just ahead. Just beyond it was some sort of cage. The wall of knots and ties acted as a barrier that either kept others out or someone or something in. How tightly the threads had been twisted. With a surge of emotion, she approached the tangled mess. Fear hung like a stench over this place – a stench that said *Keep Out*! She knew she couldn't keep out, though.

What happened next was inexplicable in the world of reason. Jedda's instincts completely took over. She knew what to do as if she'd done this a thousand times before – she knew what to do as if her life depended on it. Her hands traced the snarled knots. Following a twisted line of energy deep into the earth, she understood without understanding, what it was. Someone had harnessed the energy of the land, and inverted it. They had twisted it like a knot to serve and feed only that to which they directed it. What was worse is that this twisted knot acted as a seal that trapped something down here.

Her heart started glowing and from the center of it a rainbow poured out, following the twisted energy lines into the ground. Using sheer will and the purest intention of love, the twisted lines began to loosen. Once undone, there was nothing to keep the seal in its place. Like a valve it released, and the cage disintegrated. Hundreds of faeries and elementals that had been affected by this dam burst forth. And then there was one face, so familiar.

"Thank you. I knew you would come," he said.

"You are welcome." She was in shock. "Who are you?"

"Don't you remember?" She didn't answer, but suddenly he came into focus more clearly. "Taivyn!"

Then he was gone. An imprint from where he had been remained. It looked like a dragon.

****

She hadn't spoken for two days. She couldn't. Unable to go out, she stayed in her room. And Lou didn't push her. Just as Lou was wondering if she had made a mistake bringing Jedda here, the young girl finally voiced what had been circling like a vulture in her head since that day at the Tor.

"It's like he'd been asleep for thousands of years. His soul had been trapped there, Lou. All this time, his soul had been trapped."

"Who, Jedda?" Lou asked gently.

In all her telling of the tales of the Forest, Jedda had never shared the part about Taivyn. That part of her journey had remained hers and hers alone.

"Taivyn...," she whispered as a tear slid down her face.

Chapter 27
No One Hears Her Scream

"We call them faerie.
We don't believe in them.
Our loss."

- Charles de Lint

England – 2005

How do I make peace with myself? What is it that I am saying, speaking, writing, singing, yelling, screaming? I scream silently. And I cannot be heard. My voice is the loudest it has ever been and yet it remains silent. Why? Why has this task been given to me? One would think that time would heal this sadness I feel. I am a mix of feelings; like a torrential whirlpool they storm inside of me, vying each for my attention, for a piece of me. I am filled with joy and wonder as a result of these new and miraculous unseen worlds being opened unto me. Yes, the joy and the wonder...but then they flow into the anger and bitter confusion. Like a waterfall, a powerful moving current rushing towards a cliff as it swirls and mixes, converges with all forces before throwing itself over, tumbling, thundering, roaring! These incessant energies crash upon the rocks and then sink down into an unforgiving abyss of nothingness below. I scream again. Also unheard. Unknown. A soundless sound. A voiceless voice. I am heard by no one. I am the unheard.

Unheard by the ears of man. Unheard by the One I love. If only he could hear me without words. Could hear me for what and who I am! Why do I have to be anything? Why! Why!

S he threw her pen across her hotel room. Her notebook was soon to follow. A heap of pages landed on the floor. Jedda collapsed on her bed. A crumpled mess of hair fell around her face. Her last night in England, and she sobbed herself to sleep in the darkness once again.

Somewhere in Maine 2005

A noise in the dead of the night broke his somewhat peaceful slumber. He wrestled and thrashed before jumping to his feet. So shaken was he by what he had heard. The noise was so piercing, but more than that it moved through his entire being across time and space. He didn't know if it had come from within or without.

He looked around. It was pitch black. The light of the moon did not shine on this night. Challenged even were the stars as their twinkling light barely escaped the thickness of the trees outside his house. The only sounds seemed to be a chirping contest of sorts between the locusts and crickets. The croak of the frog seemed most distinct of all.

He squinted to see if he could adjust his eyes to make heads or tails of what he'd just experienced. Nothing seemed out of place. Although he couldn't see anything, neither could he sense any movement out of the ordinary either inside or out. He scratched his head. He was sure he had heard the scream of a young girl. Perhaps it had only been a dream.

Chapter 28
A Keeper, a Cat and a Raven

*"You won't discover the limits of the soul,
however far you go."*

- Heraclitus

Maine – 2005

Lou pulled up in her driveway, parked her car, and remained seated. What an overwhelming trip it had been. She could only imagine what Jedda must be feeling right now. She hoped that it had not been too much for the young girl. Jedda was strong, though. *The universe never gives us more than we can handle,* Lou reminded herself. Then she wondered if she were justifying what could be construed as her carelessness where Jedda was concerned. Only she did care – immensely. They had grown extremely close over the last year. She loved the girl like a daughter. Jedda didn't need a mother, though. She needed a teacher and a mentor. And that is exactly what Lou Silverton endeavored to be.

Lou thought she would give Jedda some time to process. Heck, Lou needed to process, too. The Tor of Avalantia was associated with far more than most people realized. For one, it had been the seat of ancient Faery Wisdom. There was, however, quite a bit more to the story. If the ancient prophecy had been fulfilled...Lou began to ponder the implications. One thing was certain: Jedda had awakened someone or something. Lou could sense it. She could feel the flux in the energy field of the Earth. She sighed. No longer could she put off speaking with Sonny Ramen.

It wasn't that Lou didn't want to speak with him. Any time she saw him, Lou would feel an overwhelming urge to rush into his arms and give him a gigantic bear hug, treating him like the brother she had never had. Over the last few years, however, Lou had become so hyper-focused on finding the next Keeper that her personal relationships began to suffer. Okay, truth be told, they were deteriorating like a compost pile. The search had consumed her. Looking back on it now, she felt a little ashamed that she had let it get to her the way it did. Then she thought about the wise words a cat once said to her not too long ago – something about being gentle with herself. She giggled. Isis was irritatingly accurate in her perception of Lou. And she was right, of course – Lou did need to go easy on herself. So what was she waiting for? This weekend she would call Sonny Ramen, and she wouldn't beat herself up about not having done so earlier.

She turned her thoughts back to Jedda. They didn't start back to school for another few days. She'd give her a call on Sunday. In the meantime, she needed to get organized. They'd been gone awhile and she didn't like being away from Isis for so long. Not to mention that she still had some student papers and tests to grade. She silently contemplated her list of what she needed to get done. Organization always settled her and helped her gain clarity.

Lou stepped out of the car. She grabbed her purse from the back seat, swung it around her shoulder, and shut the car door behind her. She went around to retrieve her luggage from the trunk. As she made her way toward the front door, Lou paused briefly when she spotted Isis in the window. A heart-warming smile developed. Isis must be anxiously awaiting her return so they could discuss the trip.

Still looking at Isis, Lou noticed that something was a little out of place: her cat did not even notice her. Her furry friend was fixated on something else just overhead. Lou followed the cat's gaze. She scanned the maple tree, and stopped abruptly. There on the branch of the tree sat a black crow-like bird peering down at her. Baffled, Lou looked at Isis, then back at the bird.

She knew Isis had long outgrown pursuing mice and other such creatures. It had been in her nature when she was a kitten, but as Isis got older she lost interest in stalking prey. Isis had explained to Lou that she had matured considerably, and no longer desired interacting with feeble-minded beings. She had been referring to rodents, but since then Lou had not caught her preying on anything. The cat never gave them a second thought. They just did not seem to concern her – until now. Isis had not even looked at Lou once, so absorbed was she in this winged creature.

Then before Lou could make sense of it all, an unexpected thing happened:

"Greetings, Keeper! I would like to speak with you, and your cat. I assume from the looks of her she is a Faery Cat, and therefore I should be safe as long as she finds me agreeable. I suppose you might find it a bit cold out here. Shall we go inside? We have much to discuss," the bird began.

Lou glanced at Isis. This time Isis returned her gaze. There was a silent agreement between them. Lou turned back to the raven, and offered an official verbal invitation: "You must be Yuri. We've heard a great deal about you from Jedda. Yes, of course. Do come in. Isis has agreed to be amicable. You will be safe. You have our word."

As soon as they were all comfortable, the raven spoke again, "I am pleased to finally meet you both. I am here on quite an interesting and urgent matter, having traveled longer and farther than you can possibly imagine."

Isis was not impressed. She cocked her head to one side, and stared intently at Yuri. "Try me," she challenged.

Lou shot a look at her cat, "All right, all right. Isis, you promised. Now please let the raven speak, will you? Some of us are interested in what he has to say."

Lou turned back to the raven and offered her full attention, "All right, Yuri. Go on. I do apologize for Isis. Sometimes she can be…," Lou searched for the most accurate word that would not offend the cat, "…difficult." She eyed Isis with a look that made the cat think twice before retorting with one of her usual, sarcastic remarks.

Judging by Lou's seriousness, Isis thought it best if she conceded, "Oh okay. Yes, bird. Do go on. We both are very interested in what you might be doing here, and what business you have with a Keeper. Do keep in mind, though, that we have things going on here as well that need seeing to if you don't mind, hmm?" Although she wouldn't outwardly admit it, Isis wanted to hear about Lou's trip.

With that Yuri began to reveal the circumstances pertaining to his arrival: "We are at a pivotal time within the circle of eternity, all of us. You sit on the brink of an Age of Light, whereas the time from which I hail is heading into an Age of Darkness. As you well know, things probably turned out challenged at best. Although we believe that we figured out a way to ensure that the candle remains lit, so to speak, even if it must be hidden…." Yuri allowed time for his words to settle in.

Lou knew he meant in addition to the original line of Keepers. Lou thought back to the stories that had been told about the origin of the Keepers, and the purpose of them: the Keepers were to be a golden thread that would withstand the test of time, even through the darkest of ages. Lou was living proof to

Yuri that the Line of Keepers would not fail. However, he could tell something had changed; for even though Lou exuded the same energetic signature as Lunaya, by which he was able to identify her as Keeper, he knew that the line had been affected by the darkness. There was a dullness in her field. Something had been forgotten, or worse – lost.

Lou blushed, embarrassed by her transparency, and realized that it was only a matter of time before Yuri comprehended the truth of what had happened – or from his perspective, what would happen. The raven left the subject alone. It was not his intention to upset Lou. He knew, from working with Lunaya, the burden that a Keeper bears; he sympathized, and decided against probing into this.

While it was obvious that she felt the shame of her truth burn, Lou waved it away, pretending not to be disturbed. She questioned, "You mean Jedda? Do go on, please."

The bird continued, "Well, essentially, yes. But the thing is that it is not just about 'what' or 'who' but also a matter of 'how.' You see, there is an event on the horizon that has the power to change life as one knows it!"

"You refer to the Great Deluge, then?" was the cat's inference.

Yuri smiled. He admired the sharp wit of this feline. She was no doubt a Keeper's Cat. He answered swiftly so as not to keep the cat waiting. He could tell that she did have a temperament about her.

"Yes, you are clever, O Cat of the Keeper. However, while we are aware of the Fall of the Great Nation in the Sea, it is not the Deluge that we speak of…I am here about something else…something even greater…."

Lou and Isis could not imagine another event taking precedence over the Great Deluge. Lou looked away deep in thought.

"What in the universe? What event could have more greatly affected our path in the last 13,000 years?"

The raven eyed his two hosts intently; with a twinkle in his eye he asked, "Have you heard of the Frog and the Mushroom?"

Chapter 29
It's All Connected

"When you describe such a magnificent happening, you must circle it, just as a story that is stalking you circles you. You must describe it in a circular fashion, because all life is a circle, and to reach truth we must move within that sacred circle."

- Lynn V. Andrews, *Shakkai*

Maine – 2005

Lou and Isis were confounded, and that was an auspicious event in and of itself, especially where the cat was concerned. It was Isis who broke the silence.

"So the Frog and the Mushroom, huh? That's how those of your time did it? That's how the soul that is Jedda transformed from Faery into Human Consciousness?"

Yuri sensed a genuine question. Her guard had come down considerably. It was as if that revelation had disarmed the cat slightly. Not wanting to expose his knowledge of the cat's vulnerability, he answered very matter-of-factly, "Yes, it is…or, from my perspective, it will be."

While Isis seemed to be uncharacteristically lost in some state of nostalgia, Lou took the stage with her next round of questions, "The Ancient Ones…We know that not only the destiny of the Moon Clan, but all of humankind's, is deeply intertwined with the destiny of the Faery Race. Many now do not feel their presence anymore or even know they exist."

Yuri was listening, but somewhat incredulous, "My Lady, that is hard to fathom. They would not ever leave the Earth, though. Not until they see her through. I know this."

Lou could see that he had a deep respect for these beings, which said a great deal, especially coming from a raven: "Yuri, I do not mean to upset you. And no, they would not leave the Earth. You are right. However, they live mostly beyond the Veil now."

Yuri looked as if he were deep in thought, pondering this. That was when he realized what was different about Lou: because of the seemingly severed connection with the Faery Race, or more accurately the denser vibration of the planet, the Keepers lost their ability to access the records of the trees. Lou could not read Elyrie. It was like there was a wall upon her heart, where normally there existed a clear channel through which to hear the Language of the Trees. This channel had been blocked, or possibly even severed.

Sensing that Yuri had now picked up on the root of her shame, Lou wrapped her sweater around herself more tightly, as if that would hide the truth. To her, it was an energetic scarlet letter that she wore for "all those with eyes to see" to witness her denigration. The raven could not help feeling the similarity between Lou and Lunaya. He had spent enough time with Lunaya to get to know her a bit, or as much as her guardedness would permit. The two Keepers did resemble each other in physical characteristics, but it was something more than that. It occurred to him the moment he felt the need to cheer her up. He did not want her to feel saddened. Nor did she have to feel ashamed. There was nothing she could have done to prevent it. Of course, if Lou was anything like Lunaya, he knew how critically hard on herself she probably was.

Yuri thought long and hard of what he might say next. He was glad when Isis spoke, "So bird...Yuri, right? Did you come all the way here to tell us the method by which you did a transforming trick 13,000 years ago?"

"No," was Yuri's succinct response.

Lou forgot about her source of shame for the moment. They waited patiently for Yuri to fully reveal the reason for his visit. Finally the bird added, "I came to warn you."

"Oh boy. Listen bird. We really need some positivity out of you, right now," Isis pressed.

Yuri sighed. Faery Cats. How demanding they could be! "Yes, well, I didn't want to alarm the girl, which is why I'm telling *you*. The thing is, when Rose crosses over it may affect Jedda as well. After all, everything is connected."

Chapter 30
Nothing Like an Old Friend

"I always return to the Mystery…And I think there is nothing in this world but the Mystery."

- Kenneth Patchen, *"I Always Return to This Place"*

Maine – 2005

Lou sat and relaxed into her sofa with Isis on her lap. She stroked her cat's soft fur until she heard a gentle purr. Kicking off her shoes was next on her list. A little rest was all she wanted. Yuri had said that it *could* affect Jedda. He hadn't been sure. She would need to consort with some of her peers about this – it was a little out of her area of expertise. Then again, that was the funny thing about Time – it wasn't really anyone's expertise. Either way, this would require a group effort. Lou reclined deeply and sighed. Then she noticed the red light flashing on her answering machine. Voicemails. Great. They could probably wait until later. Then she thought better of it.

Lou scooted Isis off her lap. While Lou had been gentle, the movement did not go unnoticed by the cat, who made it clear that her Keeper had inconvenienced her greatly. "I'm sorry, Isis, but duty calls. Voicemails." Lou indicated the flashing light, as she slid down to the other end of the sofa and hit the play button. The first was from an old acquaintance. The second was her dentist calling to reschedule her yearly cleaning. She settled in, jotting notes on a small pad of paper, so as not to forget anything. Then the last message played.

"Lou, it's Aunt Elda. I didn't want to worry you on your trip. I knew you'd listen to this when you got home. Please give me a call after you've rested. Not a second before…." There was an oddly long pause, then: "Lou, it's your cousin. I think he's returned."

Lou felt a shiver run down her spine. Her blood ran cold at the mention of him. She reached for the phone immediately. Before she could dial a number, it started to ring. She looked at the Caller ID. Smiling, she breathed a sigh of relief.

"Hello, Sonny? Sonny Ramen? Hi, it's so good to hear your voice…Well, thanks for asking, but honestly not so great. I'm really glad you called. I've been meaning to call…Yes, I know…Listen, would you care to meet me for a cup of tea at Marley's?…Yes, I did just get in, but I don't think this should wait. Sonny, I believe my cousin is back. Yes…Yes. Well, I'm trying not to go to pieces over it…All right, so I'll see you in about an hour. Okay. Sounds good. Oh and Sonny, I miss you. I'm really sorry it's been so long...All right. Yes...All right. Bye Bye."

****

Lou arrived at Marley's Tea House By the Sea a little early. It made her feel comfortable, in control of things. She sat down and ordered a steaming pot of black tea. She waited nervously for Sonny, wondering what she was going to say and where she was going to start. Sonny arrived on time, of course, as always. He spotted Lou tucked away in the corner booth. He took a seat across from her, but not before giving her a great big hug.

"Lou. It's been a long time since we've met or seen each other outside of school."

Lou smiled, somewhat ashamed. Then she ironically admonished herself, a reminder to be gentle with herself. Lou loved Sonny like a brother. They had grown up very close friends and had always been there for one another. Besides passing in the halls of the school at which they both taught, they had not seen very much of each other in the last few years. She supposed it was about time they finally got together. She had promised the Grandmother she'd pay him a visit, only she hadn't found the time before she had to go out of town with Jedda. In lieu of certain events, Lou wondered if putting off the visit with Sonny had been a mistake. *Well, better late than never*.

"Sonny, I'm so glad you could come. So much has happened. Miracles and things of wonder. Many completely unforeseeable. Some things as of late are cause for concern, however."

Sonny looked at her. In his eyes was comfort, trust, safety, "Lou, I cannot tell you how much I have missed you."

Lou sighed again. She knew she was supposed to be going easy on herself, but she felt like such a jerk for not having reached out to him sooner. After Lou had determined Jedda would be the next Keeper, she could have reached out to Sonny. Instead Lou threw herself into her work with Jedda. The last year of Lou's life had been dominated by the responsibility she felt to help Jedda remember her gifts but also to train the girl to take her place.

Sonny, who Jedda knew as Mr. Ramen, was one of Montgomery High's English teachers. He had been there longer than any of the other teachers. In fact, Jedda had been in his class the last two years. What she didn't know, however, was that while being an English teacher was his day job, Mr. Ramen was a highly respected member of the same organization as Lou. Sonny Ramen was a Moon Clan member. And not just any member. While he wasn't a Keeper, Sonny had gone through many of the training requirements. His interests lay in astrology, ancient history and, most of all, prophecy. Most of his time was spent researching ancient prophecies and how they corresponded to the great cycles of the Earth. Just like many of the Moon Clan family, however, he had pursued a career within the mainstream so he wouldn't become stuffy.

"Lou, tell me what has happened. Does it have to do with your most recent trip to England…with Jedda?" His long white beard rustled when he talked. Lou wondered if he would ever cut it. She supposed he liked the effect it created – wise and ancient. She chuckled inside.

"Oh Sonny. It surely does." Lou recounted the entire trip to Sonny, down to every last detail – at least the ones she understood. After she finished she asked if he knew anything about the Frog and the Mushroom. He stroked his beard. He looked at her for a long moment before answering.

"Lou, I believe I do. But tell me. When you were in England… has the ancient dragon prophecy been fulfilled?"

Chapter 31
Dark Things in the Alley

"In search of power and wealth, men have traversed the whole Earth, have penetrated the wilds, scaled the peaks and conquered the polar wastes. Let them now seek within the form, scale the height of their own consciousness, penetrate its depths, in search of that inner Power and Life by which alone they may become strong in will and spiritually enriched."

- Geoffrey Hodson, *The Kingdom of the Gods*

Maine – 2005

He walked through the rain wishing he were somewhere else entirely. Anywhere besides here would do just fine. Ever since last week, he had had this burning feeling that he needed to break free. Things looked different all of a sudden, like he had awakened from a dream, and he was seeing reality for the first time.

Vyn made his way through one of the old fishing villages near the shore. These small villages sat just outside the larger town's edge. Slushing through the puddles from a recent rain, he turned the corner of the historic little place. Vyncent liked strolling through the twists and turns of the charming colonial center. He loved walking on the seemingly ancient cobblestone streets that gave it so much character. How fortunate he was to live among such history, not unlike a setting in a storybook.

He followed the curve in the sidewalk, which took him ambling past an old alley. That's when he caught the sound of familiar voices somewhere in the distance. Curiously, he peered down the alley to see who it might be. Then he stopped in his tracks. Gus, one of the boys from his group was there, but he wasn't alone. He was talking to a strange hooded man. The hooded man turned slightly to reveal someone terrifyingly familiar. He'd recognize those crazed eyes anywhere. Malin! What should he do? He didn't want to be caught eavesdropping. At this point, however, any sudden move could bring unwanted attention his way. He quietly crouched further behind the dumpster he'd been standing near.

"Did you get the information I asked of you? About the girl?" The hooded man hissed and seethed an invisible venom that made the boy before him shudder.

"Well, I have a name…."

"A name? After all this time! All you have is a name?" The boy trembled at Malin's response. "Do you have anything else?"

"I'm sorry, Sir, but not really…."

Malin grumbled and glared. "Boy, I am losing my patience with you." He grabbed his collar, pulling the boy toward him, cutting off some of the circulation in his neck. Gus started to choke. Malin released his grip.

"You don't want to outlive your usefulness, do you?"

"No, Sir!" Gus screamed.

"Good! Then get to work. I want to know more about that girl."

"What do you want with her anyway?" Gus was frightened. He wondered how he'd even gotten himself into this mess. He was beginning to think that no amount of what the man had promised him could really make it worth it.

"Never you mind. That is none of your business! You leave that up to me. Do you understand?"

Gus stood, frantically shaking his head. "Yes, Sir!"

Malin flashed a ferocious look and growled. He stared off in the distance as if something had momentarily distracted him. Then he whipped back to refocus on his prey.

"Next time we meet like this, you better have what I have asked for."

"Yes, Sir," the boy stuttered. It was all he could manage at this point. By now Vyncent almost felt sorry for him, even if he was mostly a jerk ninety-nine percent of the time.

The hooded man started to leave. Then Gus added hesitantly, "Do you want her name, Sir?"

Malin turned back impatiently. Then he screamed, "Well...?!"

"It's Jedda...."

Then the hooded man stormed off. He was unwilling to waver in his demands, even though he knew he was going to have to do something about this himself. Gus crumbled to the ground. He was crunched up and dejected. Vyncent felt compelled to go to him, but then thought better of it. Gus had gotten himself into the mess in the first place. Besides, Malin was no-nonsense.

Vyncent turned and got up to leave quickly and unseen. He rushed by the tea house, unaware of the couple that sat in the window, looking flustered and deep in conversation about ancient prophecies, dragons and a young girl who might at one time have been faery. No, he didn't notice them at all. Vyncent ran down the side street and onto Main. He sprinted past the docks and toward the bus stop. He needed to get the hell out of here.

Chapter 32
Gorlin

*"We live on earth to celebrate our
life in unison with the universe."*

- Native American Shaman

The Forest – 11,000 BCE (4 months after GG)

Taivyn stayed for weeks wallowing in his emotions. Sadness mixed with a hint of self-pity seemed to be the going sentiment, although he often found bouts of rage suited him just as well. It was as if he had fallen into a steep dark hole with no way to climb out. There was no ledge or ladder in this dreary abyss where he abided. The light barely reached him. The weather seemed to match his mood, for instead of it warming with the spring, it darkened and grew colder. The fresh air was the only thing that eased his temperament, so he found himself wandering aimlessly in the Forest. Then, eventually, the cold would drive him back to the cottage where he would sink into restlessness.

He stayed in this state for more than a month, oscillating from one feeling to the next. Then one day, as if the Forest were perfectly attuned to his needs, the sun presented itself. Had it been days sooner, he would have cursed it for shining its light upon his wounds when they had not yet been ready to heal. However, as timing or fate would have it, it seemed to be the most serendipitous time. The rays trickled through the cottage window. As if the ball of light in the sky knew very well, that anything more than a handshake at this point would have been the utmost of an intrusion, its light fell only upon his hand that rested on the large fur-covered seat. Feeling the warmth in contrast to his dampened spirit grabbed his attention if only for a transient moment. Then, as if by magic, the light expanded, not to engulf him, because that still would have been too much, too quickly; it expanded to illuminate the space that was before him – the cottage. And what a mess it was!

For the first time in more than a month he took heed of his surroundings. Amelda would never have stood for this disorderly state. He wandered around aimlessly collecting things here and there. He cleared stuff away. Amelda hated disarray. He had always tried to pick up after himself. And here he had been living in chaos. He hadn't lifted a finger to clean a thing since she'd died.

He needed to do honor to her home. He cleaned some of the dishes that had piled high. He hadn't had much of an appetite as of late, but a month of minimal eating resulted in a hill of dishes accumulated in and around the washbasin. Thankfully the weather had been cold, or he'd have had his hands full with some unwanted guests.

He looked around at the progress he had made. Clearing away the clutter, clarity set in. The cottage had been her home. It was Amelda's presence that made it feel like home to him. Now it was just a lonely dwelling place. He would do her this last honor of tidying up her cottage in her memory. He'd gather his last few things from her cottage. Then tomorrow he would head out. There was no need for him to stay any longer.

Resolved, he looked around to see what still needed doing. Noticing that the table had quite a few items on it that Amelda had left behind, Taivyn thought to tidy it just a bit. There were parchments he'd been looking over. Unable to read them, he lifted them closer. They were in a strange tongue. A few stones with odd markings lay scattered about, too. It was just coming to mind now how peculiar this all was. It was as if she had left in a hurry; Amelda never left this many things out. He placed the stones in a pouch for safekeeping and decided to keep them with him. They seemed too important to leave laying around. Besides, he wanted something to remember her by. He rolled up the parchments and walked over to the shelf where she kept them all. As he was placing them on the stack, one fell out.

Taivyn knelt down to pick it up and stared in disbelief. There etched on the parchment was an image of a dragon! And beside it was an oval shaped stone...or an egg....

He recalled what Amelda had said to him with her last breath, words which, until now, he had compartmentalized in a little box that read "do not open until later." Unable to process the death of his friend until this moment, her last words had been received in a dream-like state, waiting on the edge of here and there. The things she had told him in those last moments…as if someone had taken that little box off some forgotten shelf and finally handed it to him, he began to recall the things she had spoken.

The prophecy! She had said he was "the last of the Dragon Clan." Thinking about the dreams, he knew the dragons were real, and he knew it was the dragons who were sending him the dreams. What had Amelda been hiding? Why had she kept this from him? Probably the usual: she wasn't sure if she could trust him. Or she had thought he was too young, too impetuous to be told such things. Another tear fell from his eyes. He didn't mind that she had secrets. Only that she was gone. He was going to miss her so much!

He lifted up the paper from where it lay on the floor and studied it more carefully. The egg was clearly not just an egg because around the shape were beam-like drawings suggesting that it glowed or radiated. He didn't know the last time he saw a glowing egg. He wished he knew exactly what this blasted prophecy that everyone seemed to be talking about really said. He wondered what it had to do with a glowing egg.

Looking even closer he now could make out the drawing of a person in the corner. There were some markings next to the person that he didn't understand.

He rolled the parchment up into a scroll, and attached it to his waist belt. This was coming with him, no questions asked. He didn't understand what it meant, but he knew it had something to do with him. He was starting to put the puzzle pieces together. Amelda had said he was part of the Dragon Clan. Taivyn remembered stories about the dragons in his classes with Ra-Ma'at. They had always fascinated him.

He finished cleaning up. Taking a bit of food, he added it to his few belongings and made a little bundle. While he hadn't been keen on food as of late, eating regularly was something he usually preferred if he could help it. Everything was placed neatly by his pallet, so he'd be ready to depart by first light. He looked the place over. Amelda would be proud of his cleaning attempt. He heated some water in the cauldron to boiling and made himself a cup of tea. He would drink to Amelda: one last tea in her cottage one last night. When the pot started to bubble he pulled it off and poured the water over a sprinkling of dried herbs and leaves. Who knows what they were, but he'd watched Amelda long enough to know what she put in there even if he didn't know the plants by names like she did.

Just as he was settling down, a *rat-tat-tat* came on the door. Someone was knocking. *Who can that be?* He really hadn't seen anyone else in the woods in all this time, except for the creatures that were pretty much left to their own devices out there in the deep Northern part of the Forest.

He ran to the door so as not to keep the visitor waiting.

"Who is it?" he called. One couldn't be too careful. He didn't sense a threat, but it didn't hurt to use a bit of precaution.

Rat-tat-tat.

He heard the sound again, but no one answered. He cracked open the door to have a look. The wind blew in, making the fire crackle and dance. He didn't see anyone there. Opening the door a little wider, a loud voice boomed through the cottage.

"Well, don't just stand there! Do invite me in!"

A short little creature with silver sprouts of hair stood in the doorway. The height of the creature accounted for his lack of visibility when Taivyn had first opened the door.

"Yes, come in. Who are you?"

"Who am I? Who are you? You are the one in the place where Amelda is not. She didn't tell me about you."

"Well, she didn't tell me about you, either."

"Hmpphh!" The small stubby creature realized they weren't getting anywhere.

"Well, if you must know I've gone by many names in my day. Some call me the Grandfather. Others refer to me using a title that conveys a bit more formality, but that won't do in this case either. You may call me Gorlin, and if you couldn't already tell, I am a gnome."

A gnome? Taivyn looked the gnome up and down, as if inspecting him. Well, he did sort of look like a gnome, except different somehow. Then again, the subject of gnomes was definitely not one in which his expertise lay. *What do I know about gnomes, anyway?*

The stumpy creature was better dressed than any of the other gnomes he had ever seen. This one wore a richly embroidered garment and cape that hung low to the ground. Upon his head, in place of the usual pointy hat, branches and bark twisted to form a crown of sorts…just like a king….

Taivyn wondered if gnomes had a king. Then he realized he hadn't responded to the gnome's introduction: "Well, my name is Taivyn and I'm a human…I think."

The gnome rolled his eyes. "But of course you are." He eyed him up and down. "A little tall, I might say…and perhaps a bit scrawny." He pulled at Taivyn's tunic to expose the gauntness that had developed as a symptom of his grief. Taivyn pulled it back, a little annoyed. "But all in all, I'd say yes, a human. Now then. We have gotten that out of the way. Who are you?"

"Like I said, my name is Taivyn."

The gnome looked at him unsatisfied. "Yes, do come off it, Boy. What are you doing at Amelda's cottage?"

"I have been staying with her for some time now, several moons."

"Several moons, you say?" the gnome eyed him suspiciously. He stretched his neck to peer around the boy. He looked to his left, then to his right. He stepped up and attempted to enter, but Taivyn wouldn't budge.

"Man, you can't be serious. Do let me in. I need to see if...."

Taivyn was adamant. "You haven't said what you are here about."

"Right, well, if you would just let me in to verify my...," and with that Gorlin used his hefty weight and pushed Taivyn out of the way. The gnome was quite large – short, but large – much more so than the gnomes Taivyn had met last year in the Forest, or the yellow-hatted one he spied around the cottage once in a while. Gorlin had a roundish sort of potbelly that looked like he'd enjoyed himself with one too many handles of mead.

Taivyn let out a yelp. He felt like this was blatant disrespect to a woman whose home they were in that had so recently crossed over to the Eternal Sea.

"Please, gnome! Gorlin! What right have you, man?"

Gorlin stormed into the center of the main room. He looked around at the sink and then to the fireplace. Then back again. "Amelda!" he called.

He called a few more times and then stood there in the center of the room staring at the hearth. A forlorn look washed over his face. Then finally, "She's gone, isn't she?"

Taivyn was a little surprised that he had made the guess. He felt he'd done a fine job of tidying the place up – Amelda-style. He was unsure of whether or not to trust this creature. Then again, playing these games was becoming futile. Perhaps if everyone just started communicating a bit more there wouldn't be so much confusion. He conceded.

"Yes. She is gone. I'm sorry. I'm so very sorry."

The wound that was so new opened again, and tears slid down the boy's face. Gorlin was deeply saddened and disturbed; the genuine reaction from Taivyn assured him that there might be more to him than some bum sneaking into the cottage to catch a few warm winks of sleep. And this confirmed that his suspicions were true. He had felt a sensation accumulating over the last months that all might not be well.

"I'm sorry, too," said Gorlin. And he was. Amelda had been a trusted ally, and a good friend to the Forest. He had respected her a great deal. He still did. They had known each other for years. He remembered her from before she...he shuddered to think what had become of her. She had been young and beautiful, as many of her kind remained for so long. She would always be beautiful, but young she was not. Not anymore. Not since....

"Do you know what happened?" asked the gnome.

"No, not really. The night before she died all was well. At least I thought it was. I went to sleep. When I awoke, Amelda was nowhere to be found. I figured she'd just gone for a morning walk or perhaps to harvest some berries or cherry bark. Alas, I did not find such to be the case. I ran all through the Forest searching for her. Finally I thought she might be over at that old well."

"Well?" Gorlin looked alarmed and very concerned. Taivyn did not notice as he was deep within the memory of what had taken place.

"Yes, the well. There's this old well just on the far Northern part of the land. It's surrounded by beautiful wildflowers and Amelda sometimes would go over there. In fact, it was where I had first met her. Under terrible circumstances, I might add."

Gorlin's interest in the boy's telling of the tale turned into a look of dreadful concern.

He could not imagine that she would have drunk from the well again, however. They had gone over the repercussions several times. And for goodness sake, her physical appearance was a testament to it! For the love of the Forest!

"Did she drink from the well?"

Taivyn didn't understand the gnome's question. Why would he care about a small detail like taking a drink from an old well?

"I don't know if she drank from the well. How would I know something like that? When I found her she was lying on the ground – just like the first time I found her. As I mentioned, that's how we met, actually, and…."

Taivyn began to recall his first encounter with the old woman. He had been stomping around through the Forest aimlessly. It was shortly after he'd met Jedda. He couldn't stop thinking about the young girl. He just couldn't get the sound of her voice, or the way her eyes sparkled when she said his name, out of his head. He had felt like he was found and lost again. He was completely out of his mind that he might never see her again. She was gone. Vanished. As if she never was. All this had been too much to bear.

It was around that time that his dreams had become more incessant. He had tried to focus on his quest, but to no avail. Who cared where he'd come from? Well, he did, but he didn't really know where to begin or what to do. He would sleep in beds of leaves or sometimes he might climb up high in the trees to rest on the branches and fall asleep. And then of course he was plagued by the dreams. They picked up with a ferocity that terrified him. The vividness and detail of these night visions increased day by day. They were different. Sometimes the landscape would shift. Some of the dreams took place deep within the Earth, while others occurred soaring through the sky. But always, almost always, there were two seemingly coherent characteristics – two elements that were consistent no matter the landscape or the time period. Those two things were the dragon and the rose.

In fact, those symbols became so pronounced he could feel them inside himself even upon waking as if they were an innate part of him. He became lost in these dreams even in waking consciousness. He began to wonder what was dream and what was reality. He would awaken and scream and thrash about. Sometimes he would wake up and just start running. He didn't know if he was running away from or toward something. He would just run.

It was one of these fits that he was experiencing when he found Amelda. He had awakened from one of the most powerful dreams yet:

I am asleep. I can see myself sleeping. The dragons are calling to me, but I do not answer. I cannot. I am too far deep. A part of me thrashes about. Wake up! Wake up! But I cannot. I am sleeping so deeply, it is almost like death. Next I notice a rose that lay at my side. Then I see her face. It's Jedda...only it isn't. I know her. I know her well. Then I watch myself awaken. I can now hear the voices of the dragons once again.

Taivyn couldn't understand it, so he ran. He just ran and ran and ran. He ran for what seemed like forever. Days and nights. He ran and came to the northern part of the Forest near an old well. That's when he found her – an old woman lying on the ground gasping for air. She was alive, but very unwell. He ran to her side.

"Madame. What can I do?" She made a gesture in the southerly direction. He picked her up and carried her swiftly, hoping to find someone along the way. They didn't run into anyone but there just ahead was a little cottage. She nodded. He ran with her in his arms into the cottage. He called out for help. She shook her head. He understood it to mean that she was alone. He laid her out on a long, soft seating area that was lined with animal furs and fabrics.

She pointed to a long table just behind them. It had an array of dried herbs and powders resting atop it.

"Medicine? Do you have something over there that I can use to help you?"

"Try the red leaves and powdered violets," she eked out from her tiny and weather-worn mouth.

Taivyn ran over to the table and thrashed around. He found the violet powder easily enough. He had more difficulty locating the red leaves. She saw his dismay.

"Under table. Little shelf," she muttered in a raspy voice.

"What should I do with it? Tea?"

"Mix in water." Her eyes closed. He was losing her. He ran over, herbs in hand, to the basin and cutting board. He got a little dish out and poured random amounts of the herbs in. Then he added some water. He looked for something to stir with and found nothing. Feeling hopeless, he used his fingers to mix the herbs in the water. He ran over to where the old woman lay and propped her head up with his free hand. Bringing the little bowl to her mouth, "Drink. Drink!" he said. He was frantic. He got most of the liquid into her mouth and made sure she swallowed it. He laid her head back down and waited. That was the longest hour of his entire life. She opened her eyes and smiled.

"You did it. What a brave little man you are!" Her voice was no longer the croak it had been when he'd found her. It was strong and fluid. Her skin seemed less wrinkled, too. What a transformation!

"The well, Boy! Did she drink from the well?" Gorlin had interrupted his recollection. He was a little agitated that the gnome insisted on this ridiculous question, and called him "boy," for that matter.

"I don't know if she drank from the well. I found her lying on the ground and...," then he remembered the silver goblet that had laid next to her. It was empty. They never used vessels such as that. Most of the ones he had seen her use were wooden or clay. He'd never seen it before except....

"There was something strange. Next to her on the ground lay a silver goblet. I had never seen her use it before. But now that I…I seem to recall that same silver goblet laying on the ground the day I found her…I never really noticed it before…."

Gorlin looked upset. "Yes."

The gnome looked disappointed and sad. His eyes seemed distant, far away, "Yes. She has drunk from the well. For the last time she has drunk from the well."

Chapter 33
Get Out Now

"Great forests must flourish, and man must see to this if he wishes to continue to live on this planet. We are, indeed, the skin of the earth, and a skin not only covers and protects, but passes through it the forces of life."

- A Leylands Cypress Deva in Dorothy Maclean*'s*
Call of the Trees

Maine – 2005

L ou had dropped Jedda off earlier that afternoon. The trip had been intense and Jedda wanted some alone time to process. She was a jumble of emotions, and she felt like crying. She hated it when others saw her cry so she had locked herself in her room. Her parents wouldn't be getting in until late that night since they had a dinner to go to after work. Except for her little brother, Jake, no one was home. This was fortunate seeing as they would have probably wanted to hear about her trip. Artemis was lying beside her as she journaled her thoughts and feelings like a royal mess of splatter paint.

She could not shake the vision she'd seen of Taivyn – or someone who looked just like him – at the Tor. It threatened to distract her, even to consume her. She gave her heart full permission to soar freely on these pages, writing all the feelings that poured out upon it. She did not stop anything. She allowed everything; the time for holding back was over. How could she feel this connection to someone she didn't even really know! The moment that thought appeared, however, she knew it wasn't true. She did know him. That was confirmed the moment she had stared into his eyes. Not knowing if she was staring into her own soul or his, it was as if she had known him forever.

A great fire burned deeply, kindled, but unattended. If not put in check it could quickly consume her. Why did it feel as if a part of her were lost? She needed to keep going, keep pondering, keep searching…for answers, for understanding, for peace. She felt paralyzed with suffering for him and what he might have endured in that trapped state.

The writing seemed to be helping a lot. Jedda was in mid-sentence when the doorbell rang. Certain that her nosy little brother would be the first to rush to the door to see who it was, she remained seated. *Let him get it*, she thought. It would give the little twerp something to do anyway. The more he had to do, the less time he had to bother her.

As predicted, Jake went scampering to the door like a little rat. He was sure he would beat Jedda. When he arrived at the stairwell, Jake realized that Jedda was not coming. Strange. She had been rather aloof when she had gotten home this afternoon. She had just gone straight to her room and hadn't come out since.

The doorbell sounded again. *Who could it be?* Jake opened the door to a looming figure before him. A strange-looking man stood in the doorway. His hair was dark and wild like a roosting duck on top of his head and he had a snout for a nose. He was oddly dressed in clothing that looked like a combination of rags and medieval garb. A menacing look was in his eye.

"Hi. Can I help you?" Maybe the man knew Jake's parents.

The wind blew hard against the man. Surprisingly he did not budge. As leery as he looked on first glance, he seemed to be immovable. He answered in a scratchy droll that sounded like he had smoked one too many cigarettes in his day: "Well, actually I was looking for someone else. Jedda. Is she here?"

"Jedda?" Jake was caught off guard. Why would the man be looking for his sister? He was much too old to be a friend. Wait a minute...maybe this was one of Jedda's teacher's. Maybe she was in trouble. Fascinating! Surely Jedda must be in trouble for her teacher to pay a visit to their home; it was not that late, but late enough that most proper teachers would not think to arrive at one of their students' homes, he thought. He had this vision of schoolteachers being the type that arrived home from school, and never left. In either case, the unsettling look that the man gave was certainly an indication of Jedda's misdeeds. A wry smile arose across the little sibling's face. This was fantastic! Serves her right, he was sure. For what he did not know, but surely for something.

Jake answered in a tone that did not belie his pleasure in submitting to the man's request, "Oh of course. She's in her room. Would you like me to take you to her?"

The man smiled a smile almost as wry as that of the young boy, "That would be marvelous. Thank you." That was all the persuasion Jake required. He opened the door wide, and allowed the man entry into their home.

****

Jedda had continued writing away when she heard the doorbell sound again. Then she heard her brother thumping through the house racing to make it to the door before her. Little did he know that she did not care the least bit who might be on the other side – until her pen did something uncanny.

Before she had time to judge the words that flowed out onto her paper there was an ominous warning before her. There, written on her paper, as if she had written it with her own hand were the words:

"DANGER – GET OUT NOW!"

What in the world? Why would she have written it? She had no rational explanation for this message. She had not felt threatened. Although now she felt a shiver run up her spine. Not knowing if it was attributed to the message or to the…she heard Jake open the front door.

Okay. She needed to be calm. Someone or something was warning her of danger. Should she really ignore it? Probably not. Besides, if it were just the product of an overactive imagination then she could laugh about it later.

Her intuition was telling her to heed the message. She could hear her brother dialogue with someone; however, she did not recognize the scratchy male voice. Jedda put on her shoes and jacket with a speed of which lightning itself would be proud. Then she made a run for it. Bolting out of her room, she dashed down the hall in the opposite direction of the stairwell, and into her parent's bedroom. There was no stopping there, though. Jedda flung open the sliding glass door that opened onto the upper deck of their patio. Luckily these two outside levels were connected by a wooden flight of stairs. She rushed down them as if she were running for her life. It was dark now, and she would have to maneuver through the yard from memory. She prayed she would not trip and fall. She hopped from one stone to another trying to stay on the path that wound through the gardens and led out to the front yard. She slid behind a bush and hid there. Her heart was racing. She felt a primal terror in the pit of her stomach. She decided to wait here and catch her breath.

Jake led the man to Jedda's room. He knew his sister was going to be pissed that he took anyone to her room, most of all a teacher. He knocked on the door to make a fake demonstration of courtesy. He called out, "Jedda, you have a visitor!"

When she did not answer, he turned the doorknob and entered. He was really enjoying this a little too much. "Jedda!" he called out as he went into her room. The man followed closely behind.

Well, that was strange. There was no one there. How could that be? He knew she had been in here; in fact, she had not come out since she arrived home. He cursed under his breath. He turned to the man: "I'm sorry. I thought she was here. I don't know where else she would be. She must've left, and I didn't realize it."

The man looked perturbed, but only for a fleeting second. He quickly composed himself, returning to the expressionless gaze. Jake continued, trying to remedy the situation. He did not like looking stupid. "Well, I could leave her a note. Or if you like I could let you know when she comes back. You could even wait…."

Then he thought about his parents' discontent upon coming home from dinner that night to find this man in their home. He tried again, but the man stopped him: "That's okay. I will return another time."

Jake shrugged, and walked out of the room: "All right then. Suit yourself. I'll show you out."

The man remained for just a moment longer. He looked around, as if sensing something in the air. Then his attention was drawn to a stack of papers on the floor. They appeared to have writing on them. He glanced over the scribbled mess and then saw it. At the end of what appeared to be a semi-normal journal entry was a message. The handwriting of the message was different, and the message was clear: DANGER – GET OUT NOW!

The man's eyes flashed with a dreadful energy. Then he thought, *So it would seem the game has begun. She is further along then I had suspected. No matter.*

He took the papers, stuffed them into his tattered bag, and left the room. He found his way down the hall and to the stairwell. Jake was waiting at the landing with the door held open. Jedda's brother was just a little too willing to help this man whom he did not know. *Perhaps,* the man thought, *I might be able to use this to my advantage.* He baited him easily: "You seem like a concerned brother. I'm worried about your sister. Is there anything you can tell me about the last few months or year even that might help me better understand what might be going on with her?"

Jake thought long and hard. He was in the perfect position to really stick it to his sister now. He had also realized she was acting strangely, but he did not know why either. Then he got a sinister idea: "Um, ya know, Mr..."

"Malin," the man responded, "My name is Malin."

"Ah yes, Mr. Malin. Ya know, I don't really know what has been going on with her as of late. I do have something that might help you though. Wait here just one moment, please."

This was it. This was Jake's big moment to sabotage his sister. He could not believe his fortuitous opportunity here. He ran to his room. Opened the chest that sat at the foot of his bed. He dug like a chicken through the many quilts that his mother had insisted be kept there. She had said she had run out of storage space, and it would not hurt him any. Well, it had

193

turned out to be a great hiding place. He tossed aside the bottom quilt to uncover Jedda's journal that he had taken almost a year ago. He had taken the time to look through it briefly, but it was just about a bunch of dreams. Nothing too exciting, at least nothing that he picked up on.

Jake pulled it out. Feeling pleased, he made his way back down the stairs and held out his hands as if presenting a gift. The man moved to take the item, and for just a transient instant the young boy hesitated. Jake was not sure why he was feeling reluctant so suddenly. Perhaps it was the way this man made the air around him seem scary. He glanced outside at the leafless trees whose twiggy silhouettes waved against the light of the moon. There was a foreboding in the way these trees moved as if they were warning him to halt what he was doing. It was too late. The man took the journal and raised an eyebrow: "A diary?"

Not so sure of himself anymore, Jake stuttered a reply, "Oh yeah, it's just a diary, but it's where Jedda used to write all her most personal secrets. I'm sure it will tell you something."

The man's frown turned into a twisted smirk of satisfaction, "Well, thank you, Jake. You have been most helpful. Your sister is lucky to have a brother such as you."

Without further words, the man turned and walked out the door. Jake stood there, dazed and confused. He wondered why it felt like he had just signed his sister's death sentence. He stared at the trees for a moment, but they had become still. A chill ran up his spine. For some reason, he hoped he never saw that man again.

Hiding behind the bushes, Jedda had just enough light from the street lamp to make out the man's face. She didn't recognize him. Jedda took a closer look and her heart skipped a beat. The man's clothing was tattered and unkempt. He started his car and adjusted the rearview mirror. Then he turned on the interior light as if to search for something. That was when Jedda's insides growled in fear. She stared at the man's eyes – Jedda did not believe in evil, but this man's eyes contained something that was closer to it than anything she had ever seen.

Jedda's heart was racing as she watched the car drive away. The terror she felt had taken on a life of its own and was gripping her from within with its claws. That wicked man's crazed glare was cast in Jedda's mind like a scar. Frozen in place by her fear, she had not moved from her hiding place. She felt out of control, as if she were no longer driving the car called her Life and instead it was driving her. She stayed in a crouching position for fear that the man might return. A malicious scent hung in the air. It lingered like the long train of a wedding gown worn by the bride of Destruction itself.

The small sliver of the moon was seemingly the only light in existence on a night as dark as this, and not knowing where else to turn, Jedda gazed at it. The night air was chilly. The disturbing energy that she had felt as a result of the unwelcome visitor was finally beginning to dissipate slightly.

From where she had been hovering, Jedda stood, her thoughts returning to the foul creature of a man that had just come to her house. Somehow she knew the man did not wish her well.

Chapter 34
The Dragon Clan

"When the first baby laughed for the first time, its laugh broke into a thousand pieces, and they all went skipping about, and that was the beginning of fairies."

- James M. Barrie, *Peter Pan*

*T*he dragons helped the earth move from one cycle to the next. The full Wheel of the Ages, roughly a 26,000-year cycle, consisted of twelve smaller ages, each being a little over 2,000 years. Half were in darkness known as the Age of Sleep, and the other half in light sometimes referred to as the Age of Awakening.

Even during the Age of Sleep, the dragons would awaken from their dreaming at the appropriate time and enter the Earth Plane. They would surround the Earth with light, weaving in and out of her etheric body, moving her ever so gently. A little tilt here, a little turn there. Gently they would wobble her into the next age where different energies would govern for the next chunk of time. And this became known as the

Precession of the Equinoxes. In ancient times it was more accurately referred to as the Precession of the Dragons, but now they liked to maintain a low profile. The turn of each age, whether great or small, required such a feat.

At one time the Earth was able to support these wonderful creatures, but as time went on the planet became heavy with the burden of moving through the ages in time and space. The Earth descended deeply into matter, and then it was that the dragons had to retreat. They thought to leave the planet, but knew She could not make it without them. She was still too young to restore balance on her own. The faeries worked hard to keep the harmony flowing in her veins, but they were much too occupied with trying to ground the stars into the stones so that She could grow and spiral up toward the heavens and remember her place there.

The dragons knew their only chance was to retreat to the Inner Planes, but even then they would need help to sustain themselves. The dragon energies were fading and with them the planet grew weaker and weaker. Finally when all hope was nearly lost, a group of pure-hearted souls stood forth and volunteered their services by offering themselves. Now this was no human sacrifice although it is from this that the idea originates. The dragons would never have conceived of such a thing. No this was about self-sacrifice in the form of surrendering to a higher purpose. So the humans offered up their blood in order that the dragons could house and anchor their energies there. This group became known as the Dragon Clan and because of what they did it allowed them the ability to be one with the dragons. They could see as the dragons, they could fly like the dragons, they could listen like the dragons (in particular to horses – dragons listened well to horses), they could watch like the dragons, and they could dream like the dragons. They were essentially one with the dragons, and it was they who possessed the privilege of being able to awaken and summon the dragons if need be!

Housing the spirit of the dragon within their physical bodies allowed the dragons to both remain on the earth and return to the surface for brief periods if they so chose.

Now it was said about the Dragon Clan that they were many; living always on the edge of time in some forgotten place. Always unassuming and low-key was their nature, for they did not wish to draw attention to the secret connection they housed in their blood. They appeared as meek farmers or passive villagers just trying to survive like everyone else. Nomadic in nature, they never stayed in the same area for long. Movement was life, and staying in one place too long could mean death, or worse. As time went on, the secret they guarded was all but forgotten to the outer world. Most only remembered the stories of the Dragon Clan like a distant memory that was sometimes whispered on the winds. Sometimes a lone traveler would return with tales of this seemingly forgotten people, thus sparking the interest in dragons once again. Many would go in search of them, but none would find. The dragon clan was a most unusual breed of people.

There were four original houses of the Dragon Clan: the Houses of Earth, Air, Water and Fire. To say that one was born into a House would be inaccurate; for birth alone did not determine one's worth. One had to be accepted. It was only in the Dreaming Ceremony at the Festival of Lights that one could be chosen by the dragons. Those chosen were bestowed with the extraordinary gift of Dreaming, but they were also blessed with something else – exceptional longevity.

Chapter 35
The Singing Mount

"However men approach Me, even so do I welcome them, for the path men take from every side is Mine."

– Bhagavad Gita, iv, 11, translated by Annie Besant

The Forest – 11,000 BCE (4 months after the GG)

The mountain rose before them strong and overwhelming. Only half the stretch up was visible, the rest being completely shrouded in a swirling ribbon-like cloud that snaked its way, upward and around, to the massive mount's summit. The peak was hidden and the way was foreboding. The unknown always left a shred of trepidation as its trail. Lunaya, Telzar and Vayu stared at this superlative formation of rock and stone.

The journey had taken them months to reach this point, for the mountain lay to the north, just east of the North Wind. It still caught its draught, almost reached out for it, proud that it could withstand the force.

"We must climb to the peak if we are to listen to the mountain's song." Vayu paused before adding, "It will be…," he searched for the right words.

He was somewhat unaccustomed to interacting with humans, as he was direct and forceful; however, lacking in compassion he was not. He thought hard on how best to describe the journey ahead, and finally concluded:

"Strenuous."

Telzar knew that what he probably meant to say was "nearly impassable." Perhaps his word choice was meant to soften the effect. Or perhaps this faery elder of the air did not have adequate experience in hiking mountains with human companions. Neither he nor Lunaya had ever attempted to climb the Singing Mount, and one who knew it would not have difficulty understanding why.

Fear and hesitancy just would not do at a time like this. The Singing Mount was the highest peak in all the land. It was the one place where all the winds converged, and it was in this gathering of forces that the unknowable became known. The winds of east, south, west and north rested here atop the Singing Mount's pinnacle and told their stories to him. If one might be so fortunate to be privy to this storytelling, then what secrets they could learn! Of course it was under Vayu's direction that these winds rode and flew, but the stories were only for the mountain. It was the great gift the winds offered to the Great Stone One for letting them rest. As the winds told the stories to one another and to the mountain, they created the most extraordinary symphony of angel fingers strumming strings of silken light.

About a third of the way up the mountain, Vayu was beginning to admire his two human companions. Lunaya was strong-willed. She was stronger than he'd ever known any human to be. He had never spent much time with her, as he was much more of a big-picture kind of being. He couldn't get bogged down in the minutiae of it all. He needed to soar the wind and contemplate the heavens. Lunaya was into the details, and she was good at it. She never half-did anything, and this climb was no exception. She had not accepted defeat when the blizzard came upon them out of nowhere. Vayu could only redirect the bulk of its brunt force, but he could not alter it entirely. A storm was only half his doing. As everyone knew, the Water Clan had its fair share of responsibility in most storms that blew in. No one ever thought of that clan as being the culprits, but it was. It was indeed.

Vayu smiled as he thought of Seamone in her watery kingdom. Her domain was the Island Under the Sea. It had a name. It did. He knew it once. Lanuria. Yes, that was it. The faery island that sunk like a treasure in the ocean. One would not find her there at home, however. She'd still be with Elysinia if he had guessed correctly. Vayu sighed and the wind blew gently, rustling the strands of Lunaya's delicate golden locks.

He would not have been able to reach Seamone in time to stop the storm. Not even if he rode on the wind. They had to do their best to stay the course and hope that Lunaya and Telzar were strong enough. Well, they were strong enough, and perceptive, too. Telzar had managed to find a cliff dwelling tucked away in a pass. Vayu didn't know how he could have possibly spotted it. It was concealed adeptly. When they had arrived inside Telzar worked with the fire elementals to start a small fire. The large boulder that they slid into was enough to block most of the wind, and so they had a small blaze going soon enough. Vayu stared at them.

"I didn't realize humans were so capable. I...I didn't realize...I'm sorry."

Telzar didn't understand what all the fuss was about:

"I found the dwelling because of my time with the Rock Trolls. If it hadn't been for them, I wouldn't have noticed it. It's nothing, really."

He had no idea why anyone would ever want to spend time with the Rock Trolls. How boring they were and how slowly they moved!

"I just meant that with everything. Everything I've watched you both do. Telzar, I have watched you withstand so much. Lunaya, you have so much will, so much determination. You remind me of the wind."

The last sentence he'd spoken was a reference to his beloved, Vayanna. Not all of the faeries remained in the Forest anymore. It was the way. As the Sleep Cycle approached, many of their kind had retreated to the Land Beyond. The Forest was a borderland, a place that existed between the two worlds of Human and Faery. It acted as an entrance point, but it was not their realm.

It was almost time to return to the Faery Mists just beyond the Veil. Many waited as long as they could, but the time when they could easily move between the worlds was coming to an end. The energies were becoming denser, making it more difficult now. They would not leave the Earth, but it would seem that way, at least for a time.

Lunaya sensed Vayu was deep in thought, as so often the wind is. And a keen observer was she, deeply intuitive.

"You miss her?"

Caught off guard, "What? I...I...don't know what you're talking about. I'm unaccustomed to someone encroaching on my private thoughts!" he snapped.

She was a little hurt, but understanding nonetheless, "Vayu, forgive me, but I didn't mean to intrude. However, it's written all over your face. Listen, you don't have to continue this journey. You can go to her. Why wait? Telzar and I can do this, you know."

Somehow he wasn't so sure. Besides he'd made an oath. He was going to see this thing through. It wasn't just the journey to the peak of the Singing Mount that was important, but this whole event. If there were anything he could do to support the Earth Mother as she entered this new phase of her life, then he wanted to do it. Gaia would be turning in to take her long-appointed nap, and all who were able needed to stand watch, so that she safely made it through the night. Lunaya wasn't the only one with steadfast determination.

"I know. But I choose to remain. The wind and the light honor me with their company. This is something I need to do – for the good of the whole, for my people and for yours."

As the words left Vayu's mouth, it occurred to him that up until that very moment, he hadn't been concerned about the fate of the human race. In fact, like Leori, he had started to give up on them. Leori had not really cared whether they wiped themselves out or carried on like the miserable specimens of sentient creatures they were becoming. Weak and easily turned by greed and power, destruction was what they had proven they were most capable of and likely to do. They'd shown this to be the case time and again. Vayu had not been so quick to judge, and yet he had seen enough over the course of the last few years that had started to change his mind.

Just when he had mostly let go of all hope for humankind, here were two humans who demonstrated something different. Telzar was proving to be a fine example of the human race. And Lunaya exuded qualities for which they should all strive.

Then he became melancholy over the thought that the veils had to close for a time. For the faeries it would seem like a blink of the eye, but for the humans it would be an eternity and many thousands of life cycles. At least humans had that luxury, to come back over and over, until they got it right. Although he wasn't convinced that they would ever get it right. Well, they would have 13,000 years to figure it out. Again a hint of sadness swept over him. They would feel so alone. If they felt alone now, they would surely fall deep into the abyss of seeming separation. How piteous!

"Vayu, I think the storm has passed. Come on. You've looked deep in thought for hours now. Don't overthink things. Let's just stay focused on the task before us," Telzar admonished gently.

He had to laugh – a human telling him to stay focused. Perhaps the tables really had turned, or perhaps they were still dancing between the worlds where things were never what they appeared to be.

They climbed out of the cliff dwelling that was nestled on the mountain's side. By now they were a little less than halfway there, but they could already start to make out the peak. The dazzling colors of the winds that came to rest there betrayed its location. Unperceivable still were the distinct songs born of the winds as they told their stories to the mountain.

"Hark! Who goes there?" a voice demanded as they rounded another harrowing switchback. There was no form to discern.

Vayu stepped in front of Lunaya and Telzar, unruffled by the threatening tone.

"It is I, Vayu, elder of the Air Clan. I travel with Lunaya and Telzar of the Moon Clan. We journey to the peak of the Singing Mount. Unveil yourself!"

The wind blew as an exclamation to Vayu's statement. He unsheathed his sword used not to fight, but to illuminate the truth of the matter. Then suddenly an answer was heard in reply:

"You need not unveil the sword, My Lord. It is I, Wilma, of the Tribe of the North Winds. I bid you welcome."

Vayu and Wilma exchanged friendly salutations. After introductions were made, Vayu said, "I thought we might be approaching your domain, but not so soon. What are you doing this far down the mountain?"

"Why, My Lord, I could wonder at what you are doing so far up the mountain. You rarely come to these stark parts. Thought you more preferred the summer breezes these days. I'm told reports of you growing gusty," Wilma chuckled.

Two long, red braids, one on either side, blew to and fro as a diadem, in the form of a simple silver ringlet, glistened as it mirrored the light of the sun and the moon. Like all of the High Faeries, Wilma was tall, and her skin shined brightly with the brilliance of the Seven Sisters in the night sky. She wore a capable outfit comprised of an indigo bodice and a cape of silken white and bluish light that hung about her stark shoulders. Preferring this type of dress to the traditional courtly garb of the High Faeries, Wilma seemed to follow the beat of her own drum.

Vayu couldn't help but laugh over her comment. They were old friends. She had been his second, and he had mentored her for many centuries. Wilma joked that he was going to live forever and only kept her around for his amusement. She was not content to follow in someone's footsteps; even the respected likes of him. She rose through the ranks and when there was naught else for her to learn she left and formed a tribe of her own. Of course they still operated within the auspices of the Wind Clan, and in particular under the king and queen, or elders as they preferred to be called.

"You still haven't answered my question, Wilma…why are you so far down the mountain?"

A white bird landed on Wilma's shoulder and let out an otherworldly sound that was both song and cry.

"Thank you, Shara. I am aware." Wilma nodded and the bird flew away. "Shara has informed me that my suspicions are correct. You are being tailed. Come, we've little time. Follow me."

They raced up the mountain, rocks tumbling down as they climbed. Who could have followed them? Vayu hadn't sensed anyone. The rules of the game were somehow changing. The universe was unraveling.

"Quickly now. Here." Wilma pointed to a small cleft on the side of the mountain.

"How are we going to conceal ourselves in that?" Lunaya wondered aloud.

"Wait. Watch…," was all Vayu said.

Vayu held up his sword. A white light issued forth from its point. Then Wilma raised her arms. The cape she wore rose and blew, and a fearsome wind seemed to escape from its folds. The wind mixed with the light from the sword and a thousand fractals gleamed and burst out of nothing. From somewhere other than here an ice blue sheet of light emerged and covered the cleft. Then they stood perfectly still and waited.

****

The Dark One passed over them. Like claws his hands dug into and gripped the rocks as he slithered up the slope. He did not pay heed to the ones who stood hidden from sight as though they were invisible. As he forced himself through the nooks and crannies, the mountain scowled at the thought of such a detestable soul scaling his wall. The mountain gathered strength from the wind and sea, as mountains often tend to do. He shook with all his might; an avalanche of wind, rock and snow fell from the highest peak. Tumbling over cliffs and chasms, nooks and buttes, the icy rock trampled all in its path. The Dark One lost his footing and slid down the mountain's side. It would seem, however, that luck was on his side, for he managed to grab hold of some hook-like stone that jutted out. The Dark One dangled from it like a worm.

Meanwhile, the three that stood within the cleft braced themselves for the thunderous impact of the falling rocks. While invisible to the Dark One, they would not be safe from the forces of nature. The four looked at one another. In silent understanding they agreed to join hands. Their heart chakras lit up, connecting them one to another. Suddenly a gust of wind rose within the center of their circle. It swirled into a funnel cloud that lashed and raged.

In unison they spoke the words aloud, "We thank the Spirits of the Wind for helping us now!"

The tornado was unleashed, and just in the nick of time. It met with the crashing boulders head on. The impact caused a change of course only milliseconds from landing on the place that they stood. They breathed a sigh of relief and silently sent gratitude to Great Spirit. The mountain shivered. He had not intended to put the four in danger. It was something like an apology, only it wasn't, for a mountain does not regret. A mountain has strength and will. A mountain acts as a mountain sees fit. And the Dark One would not reach the top. It was sacred and holy ground, unfit for the likes of him.

Vayu was hopeful. Not because of his own work, but because he knew this was why they had to continue to do everything they could to maintain a connection with the humans. The faeries alone were not capable of change. They could not change the course of things once set in motion. Only humans could do that. They could move with the natural rhythm of things. They could bring harmony to something out of balance. They could not, however, use intention to change anything. He knew it was only in partnership with the humans that change could be brought to the planet. The humans must remember!

"I see you got yourself a couple of fine humans here. Thank goodness. I was almost convinced that the ones with heart had gone extinct! They are becoming such a drab bunch these days!" Wilma snorted.

She was a tough cookie, that one. Beneath that hard veneer she had admired humankind for the strength of character she knew humans had once possessed. She, too, was saddened over the demise of the race – or at least the degeneration in consciousness. Little did the faeries know how much more the race would degenerate.

"Come on! Let's go! We've wasted enough time. Look!"

She pointed to where only minutes ago the Dark One had hung. Now only the jutting hook on the side of the mountain remained. Did he fall? Or had he managed to pull himself to safety? Wilma pointed to an overhang just a few feet above them.

"We need to make it to there. That is where the entrance is."

The interior of the mountain, Vayu thought. *Of course!* The faery elder was glad for the brilliance of his protégé. Give him wind and air any day, but land, rock and mountain was mostly a mystery to him.

They scrambled to the overhang that Wilma had indicated from below. When they arrived there was nothing there. No opening or entryway that they could see.

"Wait for it," Wilma cautioned anxiously. From underneath her cape, she pulled a u-shaped string instrument. She ran her fingers across its strings, gracefully coaxing it to evoke its melody. As it started to play, she whistled an enchanting tune to accompany its already unimaginable sound of beauty. The wind blew and flickered like stars in the night sky.

"Lyra!" Vayu gasped.

Wilma only smiled. She did not respond. They waited. And then the mountain moved.

The mountain shook from the inside out. A passageway materialized. Wilma signaled for them to follow her. Once they entered, a stone slid over the opening. Vayu stared in disbelief.

"The Singing Mount and I have grown quite close," was all Wilma said in answer to Vayu's obvious wonderment. She placed her hand on one of the protruding pieces of stone within the passageway. Then the cavern lit up from within, revealing walls embedded with crystals of all colors, shapes and sizes. They produced a light that shimmered and danced off one another. Images of the Dark One climbing up the mountain appeared in the many facets.

"The Crystal Cave. I never knew it was here." Lunaya was enchanted by the sparkling scene that had come alive before her.

"It isn't," responded Wilma.

"Huh?" Lunaya did not understand.

"It's everywhere. In every mountain. The Crystal Cave is their heart and soul. It's what connects them all, one to another," Vayu had answered before Wilma had the chance. He continued, "It still doesn't explain what made you want to settle here, Wilma. Why the mountain?"

Wilma grinned, "I've been busy. But I'll explain later. For now let's get moving. Walking within the mountain will be much safer than climbing its outside walls. Might even be faster. We'll break about three quarters of the way."

"But what about the Dark One?" Lunaya was concerned. She hadn't recognized him. "Do you think he came here to stop us or is there another reason?"

"Don't worry. The mountain will take care of him. He will never let the Dark One reach the top."

Vayu's eyes lit up, giving off the light of a million stars, "The storm! It was the mountain?"

"Yes, the mountain has had eyes on the Dark One since the beginning. It waited patiently as mountains tend to do. Then when the timing was right, it began to strike. The wind is a great friend to this mountain. An unlikely match, it's true, but they are in partnership nonetheless."

Then within the shadows of the tunnel, a light grew bright. A whistling was heard through and through. The wind blew as three figures materialized. Not as easily seen as Vayu and Wilma, their forms were backlit; other than their silhouettes, they could not be clearly discerned.

"My Lady, the mountain shakes and quivers. He does not like the Dark One to tread on his holy ground. He intends to lead him astray. We would help the mountain accomplish this feat. Would you give us leave to assist in this?"

"As you wish. Go. Go and do not cease until the Dark One is stopped. He must not be allowed to reach the mountain's peak."

Like lightning and wind they departed, leaving no sign they'd once stood in the passageway. Air sylphs were beautiful creatures, but quite hard to pin down.

After traveling for most of the day, the company arrived in a dome-shaped cavern. Gold and silver patches lined the walls; this mountain was rich in both. The dome was almost geometrical in form, mimicking a five-sided polygon. Draughts blew in and crossed at the top, creating an intersection – a doorway to another world.

"What is this place?" Lunaya was enthralled that such a place even existed.

"It's called the Temple of the Crosswinds. As above, so below; as without, so within. It mirrors the Meeting of the Winds that occurs on the mountain's peak."

Telzar and Lunaya marveled at the sight. The winds twirled in song and color. It was as if their colors painted the songs. Like a gyrating circle, Lunaya turned and turned. She couldn't take her eyes off the display. How long had this occurred, she didn't know. It was a wonder of the world, if ever she did witness one.

"How long have the winds been coming here? I thought the mountain has been known as the Singing Mount for hundreds, some say even thousands of years...," Telzar conjectured.

"And so it has."

Just then Lunaya truly began to comprehend how long the faeries actually lived. She'd always known it rationally, but never really grasped it until that moment.

Wilma continued, "The mountain could not sing without the winds, and the winds could not sing without the mountain. It is the way of things."

They settled on the ground. Telzar started a fire to keep them warm. The faeries didn't require such things, but the humans sure did. Telzar reached into his bundle and pulled out a long woolen blanket that he wrapped around Lunaya. The currents whooshed through the Temple of the Crosswinds both fiercely and gracefully. Really it depended on their moods, which they changed as much as anyone.

Lunaya thought of the Dark One and the eerie feeling that crept through her when he'd passed over them. As if reading her thoughts, Vayu mentioned, "It is twisted, inverted power. It does not originate from the Earth, or from the Divine. It comes from something else."

"Now who's invading thoughts?" Lunaya jested. She didn't really care. She had nothing to hide.

Wilma had difficulty imagining the "something else" that Vayu referred to: "But how could there be something else outside of what is? I don't understand."

"Neither do I. But you two do, don't you?" Vayu looked at Telzar and Lunaya.

Lunaya offered, "Yes, unfortunately I do. As humans, we learn to tow the line. We are more physical, which means the energies we work with are quite different."

Telzar explained further, "Because of the density of our experience, we also have a choice. We can work with the Law of One, or we can deny it. If we choose to deny it we must draw our power from self. But it is an illusion, because there is nothing besides Source."

Lunaya went on, "Yes, it gets tricky, you see. The point is that the more we move away from Source the more we trust in a power outside of All That Is. It's false and doesn't really exist."

Beginning to understand, Vayu finished the thought: "But you have to believe it does. So you feed it more and more power. Until you forget that it isn't real. That is when you lose control."

Wilma cautioned, "The forces of nature can be worked with and guided...or...they can be commanded.

It is something that is never advised. And it will always backfire eventually. Eventually you become a slave to that which you command. Eventually it will command you."

Lunaya took out some fruit and nuts from her pack. Vayu had brought a flask of fruit wine. Bread and cheese were provided by Telzar. When they were settled in, and happily munching, Vayu commented, "Wilma, I am enchanted with how you have grown."

Wilma answered, "I did as you instructed me to. I listened to the stars teach me of the wind. They gifted me with this."

She held up the lyre. Vayu stared in wonder. Lunaya and Telzar listened carefully, but were clearly not so impressed.

Vayu understood their confusion and clarified, "That is not any lyre. That is the lyre of Lyra in the night sky. It is known to produce a sound so great that…"

"Stones moved, rivers changed direction and trees were charmed into dancing," Wilma finished his sentence.

Vayu wondered, "But Wilma, you are of the wind."

"I am still of the wind. What I have come to understand is that the lyre and the wind are one. It is not the sound that moves the mountains. It is the wind that the sound produces that does."

Vayu nodded approvingly. She was a being unto herself now. She had learned to shine.

Chapter 36
The Song of the Winds

"The ancients, of course, accepted the kingdom of nature spirits without question as a fact of direct vision and experience. The organs of perception of the supersensible world have atrophied in modern man as part of the price to be paid for the evolving of the analytical scientific mind. The nature spirits may be just as real as they ever were, though not be perceived except by those who can redevelop the faculty to see and experience them."

– Dorothy Maclean, *To Hear the Angels Sing*

The Forest – 11,000 BCE (4 months after GG)

A dazzling setting sun greeted them, as they climbed with the last ounce of everything they had. Vayu and Wilma were not physically exerted, but emotionally it had been a great undertaking. Until this last moment, the faery elder hadn't known if a human was capable of making this climb, even if they were a

Keeper and an elder of the Moon Clan. *Elder...what a silly word to describe a human*, Vayu thought.

They paused long enough to catch their breath and behold the breathtaking views before them. Gold and orange sank just behind the mountain's peak. Red splashed the canvas of light, so exquisite only a miracle itself could have painted it. The beauty was unrivaled and transient. The rich colors gave way to a soft violet and pink light. The azure curtain opened to allow for twilight to dance onto the stage. Floating like sentinels, several clouds guarded the mountain. The Song of the Winds could be discerned ever so softly.

Not yet to the very top, they pressed on, anxious to arrive by nightfall. Then thunder struck a chord on the clouds that turned them from white to black. The Song of the Winds changed its melody, and the party came to an abrupt halt.

"Another storm?" asked Lunaya, wondering how the weather had changed so quickly.

"I don't think so," Vayu sounded uneasy.

Then, with the dawning of the realization, Wilma yelled, "Come! We must get to the top at once. In spite of all our efforts, it seems the Dark One has found a way to get to the Singing Mount's peak."

The mountain roared its disgust for such an evil presence treading on its surface. Who was this intruder who dared to seek the stories of his friends, the winds? The Dark One stood bold and leering. He watched closely the winds that came to rest there. He listened to their songs. Then a thread caught his attention; he focused intently. The nature spirits in a hundred-mile radius cringed. The clouds clashed and burst. But the winds could not stop, for it was in their nature to sing and tell their stories. They would not change their way, not for anyone, and so they continued. Much to the mountain's dismay, the Dark One seemed to have found what he had been looking for.

The four hastily scaled steps and stones, rushing up the final few feet of the mountain's south side. At the same time the sylphs blew and whirled up from the North. They stormed the mountain's peak, but alas, they were too late.

The Dark One now turned to all of them long enough to reveal his identity, for he no longer cared to be concealed. The others gasped and cried. Then suddenly he vanished, and in the place where he stood nothing but a black crater of ash and soot remained.

"Maob...I should have known. I just...." Lunaya was furious.

"You wanted to give him the benefit of the doubt. We all did." Telzar felt as angry and betrayed as Lunaya.

"Well, he certainly wasn't here to stop us from learning his identity. He practically broadcasted it!" Lunaya rarely lost her calm demeanor, but tonight she did. "So what the hell did he want, then?"

The mountain roared and rumbled. Rain started to fall in large splashes, as if seeking to cleanse the darkness away.

"A weakness. He wanted to learn of a weakness," said Wilma as she listened to the mountain tell its story.

"A weakness? Whose weakness?" Telzar questioned.

A blanket of dread hung on the mountain like a stench. "The boy's…he came to learn the weakness of Taivyn Green," answered Vayu.

Chapter 37
Is It Really You?

"The angels suggested that we tune into Nature until there was a love flow, saying the natural world responds to our state of being, to what we are, not to what we say or do."

- Dorothy Maclean, *To Hear the Angels Sing*

Maine – 2005

J edda ran to the bus stop. She only had to take one to get to Miss Silverton's. It would practically leave her at her teacher's doorstep. Well, she'd still have to cross the park.

She greeted the bus driver and made her way to the back. Head down, not really wanting to start a conversation with anyone. Not now. Not after something like this had happened. Her thoughts went to the strange man that had been at her house. *Who the hell is he?* Jedda had not heard what the man had said to Jake, but she had a feeling he had been looking for her. She thought about his eyes – terrifying! *Who in the world has the right to be that scary?!*

Jedda looked around at the people in front of her. She felt so disconnected from most people these days anyway. She hoped none of them talked to her. Jedda was not in the mood for mindless chitchat. *It's mostly bullshit anyway!* Then she scolded herself for being so inwardly rude. Since when was she high and mighty? And who was she to take away from someone's happiness? If talking about nonsense made someone happy, then good for them! She felt the aloneness settling in again. Sometimes she wished she could talk about nonsense and be fulfilled. But she couldn't. Not when you'd experienced the kinds of things she had.

Someone behind her was making an awfully lot of noise. They were rummaging around for some papers or something. Sounded a lot like her when she was in mission mode. She chuckled. Might as well take a peek and see who on Earth could be imitating her. She needed some amusement anyway for the next fifteen to twenty minutes or so. She turned around gently so as not to make it obvious.

What?! What in the world? She whipped back around so quickly she must have looked like a superhero in full action. How could it be possible? She turned back around quietly. She studied the person still seated there – emerald green eyes, sandy brown hair, medium build. He looked just like…but it couldn't be. Still fumbling with a stack of papers, he gave little notice to the fact that she was looking at him and had been for at least a full minute.

Jedda swallowed hard. Then with all the courage she could muster, "Taivyn...? Is that you?"

The young man stopped long enough to answer her question, "I'm sorry, Miss. You must have me confused with someone else. My name is...."

He trailed off because in that moment he had lifted his head and his eyes met Jedda's stare. Something flared within him that felt like heaven and hell if ever there was such a conglomerate of emotions.

"I'm sorry. Do I know you?"

"Well, I thought so. You look just like someone that I know. Or used to know. I haven't seen him in some time now. But it doesn't matter. It's silly anyway. You're clearly not him. And anyway, he's not from around here."

"Well, you look really familiar. What school do you go to?"

"Montgomery High...you?"

"I'm a senior, but I'm enrolled in an online homeschool program now. What grade are you in?"

"Junior. I'm sorry. What's your name?" Jedda asked quickly when she realized with embarrassment that she was still gawking.

Vyn answered immediately, "Excuse me. I'm so sorry. How rude of me not to introduce myself! I'm Vyncent. My friends call me Vyn, though."

Jedda couldn't help but notice how similar he was to Taivyn. It wasn't just his physical appearance, which was a striking resemblance – almost identical, actually. His demeanor was similar, too. How odd. *But how can that be?* Tiny sparks of electricity flooded her body.

Her faced flushed hot, then cold, then hot again. She breathed deeply, hoping that he did not notice her flustered reaction. Then she realized she was taking much too long to respond in turn and quickly followed:

"Well, my name is Jedda. It's nice to meet you."

Jedda? Where have I heard that name before? Vyn tried to recall. He relented, unable to remember, and said, "Jedda. What a lovely name." Then he added nervously, "So tell me something funny." Vyn looked at her with a smile that was both mischievous and sweet.

"Something funny? I…what do you mean? You don't just meet someone and ask them to tell you something funny. And besides I'm not sure humor is my strong suit. Sarcasm maybe, but not humor."

Vyn felt ridiculous. What the hell had come over him? The last week he just had not been himself. He didn't know what had changed. He had felt free, unburdened. Even his reaction to the conversation he'd witnessed in the alley was unusual. Why would he care if Malin were meeting with Gus in secret? And yet he did. Something about it felt so wrong! He stared into the blue eyes of the young woman that sat before him. Why did he feel as if he'd known her all his life? A lump that had been forming in his throat suddenly got bigger. His heart was racing so rapidly that his chest appeared to be convulsing. And why in the world had he just made such a ludicrous request to this girl?! Tell him something funny?! What was wrong with him?

"I see. I am so sorry. You have just totally caught me off guard. And well…," the truth seemed to be the only thing to say: "I'm sorry. I'm just really having a lousy day." Vyn looked burdened,

"Tell me about it." Not surprisingly, Jedda could relate.

Jedda felt bad, and Vyn's sincerity made her want to lighten his load. Now that she thought about it, he had looked particularly flustered when she spied him thumbing through those papers. She wasn't really sure what to do.

"So where are you off to this evening? Do your parents let you ride the bus alone at night? I mean after all, you are only a junior. And you're a girl."

"Oh really. What gave me away?"

Vyn stopped, caught off guard. Jedda waited. Then they both burst out laughing.

The bus driver yelled out: Mayfair Park!

"That's my stop. I need to go. But it was nice meeting you," Jedda said, sad she had to get off the bus so soon. Jedda didn't want to leave. And although she was trying her best to muffle it, she felt the same rippling effect as when she was with Taivyn – the kind where the stars feel like they're falling out of the sky and going off within you.

"Yeah, same here! I hope to see you around again soon," Vyn replied, trying to hide the consuming disappointment he started to feel at the thought of her leaving. What was this feeling he was having with this girl right now? He'd never experienced anything like it. He was sure his girlfriend would quite object, but somehow he didn't care. He scolded himself. How terrible! What was wrong with him? He wasn't this type of guy. He definitely wasn't some hopeless romantic. On the other hand he certainly wasn't a sleaze ball either. What the hell was his problem? Falling to pieces over a girl he'd just met on a bus.

She had hoped he'd ask to accompany her. Taivyn would have. Vyncent however, had not. She'd hoped he would at least have asked for her phone number so she could see him again. Of course she had no precedent for that with Taivyn, seeing as he existed in a different world and a different time completely.

And there were no telephones in the Forest. At least she hadn't seen any. She gripped the steel bar to steady herself as she climbed down the bus steps to get off. She turned to catch one last glimpse of Vyncent before he was out of sight and out of mind. Her eyes met his. They shared a moment that might have lasted the time it takes for Jupiter to revolve around the Sun three times.

The bus driver reminded her there were others on the bus, too: "Are you going to get off, Miss?"

Jedda snapped out of her seeming trance and looked at him. She apologized and wished him a good evening. Then she jumped down and out. She stood on the curb dazed and confused. *No, no, no! Not again. I won't let this happen again*, she thought. *You can't just go around getting your heart stolen by any boy that gives you attention.* Somehow she knew that wasn't the case, though. Hell, she'd hardly given most of them a second look even when they did initiate conversation. Jedda sighed. Why did this feel like history was repeating itself? She hoped this wasn't going to be a consistent theme.

****

Vyncent was dumbstruck over his emotions. He watched Jedda get up to leave. He traced her movements with his gaze, not wanting to miss a single second. He hoped like hell that she'd turn and look at him. Just one last time. *Turn around. Let me see your eyes one last time.* Then as if she'd heard his thoughts, she did just that.

She turned to catch his gaze. He might've been embarrassed in another situation. To have been caught still staring at a woman was definitely not cool. But he didn't care. Not this time. Not today. And not with her. The bus driver made some comment to her, surely rushing her off the bus and with it Vyn's happiness, his joy, his pleasure. Damn driver. Couldn't he see something was happening here?

He stayed on the bus and wondered. Then the bus came to its next stop. Suddenly he couldn't help himself. Impulse took over completely. Vyn jumped up from his seat, and ran down the stairs and out of the bus. He didn't stop there. Vyn took off running. He ran and ran, as if nothing else in the world mattered. He'd have almost a mile, but that was okay. He had to catch her.

Chapter 38
The Serpent of Light

"...I realized that without trees, there would be no 'Mother Earth.' Earth, air, water, and fire – these basic elements – come through trees."

- Jean Shinoda Bolen, *Like a Tree*

The Forest – 11,000 BCE (4 months after GG)

The Forest sang to the faery its ten thousand songs. Upon the branches sat the blue and yellow birds, sweetly chirping their hearts content. She stood softly gazing. The birds. She would miss the birds.

"You aren't leaving the birds, you know."

"I know. I do know. But I don't think I will hear them the same way. I want to stand here as long as I can. So that I can always remember."

Elysinia smiled her understanding. She was filled with light and hope, but also sadness. She loved her so much. She didn't want her daughter to leave. Yet she knew it was to be.

"Do you know what to do?" Elysinia asked. Her question referred to crossing the Rainbow Bridge of Light that they would soon build.

"Yes, I think so. As much as I am able. It will look strange and yet familiar. And I must feel my way across with my heart."

"Yes, that is what I understand, too," Elysinia said. "It will be time soon."

Rose folded down inside the large white blossom. Its scent was sweet and intoxicating, even to their kind. She allowed the soft aroma to penetrate her senses. Releasing any will of her own, Rose relaxed into its delicate petals. She cried for the loss of her life with her Faery Kind. Most of all she cried for the loss of her beloved, for it would seem that she would not see him this time around. She had waited so long for his return. She waited still. She feared that when he finally arrived, she would no longer be here to greet him. She could feel the life she had here receding. Ever since the choice had been made, the energy began to withdraw from this world.

Elysinia watched her daughter slip gently into the blossom. As much as she wanted to remain in Rose's company, Elysinia left her alone. She knew her daughter's heart and she knew solitude was what she desired now. Over the last decades Elysinia had cherished each and every moment with her daughter. While the announcement of what Rose intended to do was shared at the Great Gathering, this idea had been long in the making.

She gazed lovingly one last time at the flower that held the one she loved as much as the stars in the sky. Rose needed to feel her own strength now as well as her own comfort. To cross over into human form from faery consciousness had not been done before. Of course, there were others who would follow in her footsteps, but it would be Rose who would lead the way. Rose was strong and determined, but she was also gentle and full of light. Now they were all counting on that light to carry her forth. Although they would be together in spirit, they would not be together like this again. The faery mother disappeared into the shadows and trees of the Forest.

Just then Elrin appeared on the side of the large hawthorn tree. "Sister, how do you fare?"

Elrin was Rose's older brother by several hundred years. A bluish white sheen always graced his skin, making him unique in this way. His hair was the color of roasted chestnuts and smelled of smoked fir. He was tall and stately, like all of his kind. A golden blue cloak hung from his shoulders. As her brother, Elrin would've chosen to accompany Rose, but he knew it was not his destiny to do so. Elrin endeavored to one day join the Faery Council. Besides Gwen would eventually join her. Guinevere had been Rose's dearest friend for hundreds of years. Long ago Gwen had made it very clear that she desired to experience human consciousness if ever there were a way.

Rose poked her head out of the flower blossom to see her brother standing before her.

"Oh everything is just swarming. Swarming in my head. I know I need to continue, but I don't know how." Her honest heart poured out its secrets.

"Go to the Great Oak before you leave, Sister. Let it show you what is to come. Let it show you the Rainbow. Then you will see the Serpent of Silver Light."

"The Serpent of Light?" Rose asked in surprise. "The dragons? But they have not awakened just yet. If I survive the crossover, who knows how long I might live? Humans have such fleeting lives these days. I may not live to see my beloved this time around."

"I wouldn't be so sure."

Chapter 39
To Reveal or Not To Reveal – That Is the Question

"They were walking in the darkness, with the shadows round them and the night's loneliness above them, through Pluto's substanceless Empire."

- Virgil, *The Aeneid Book VI*

The Forest – 11,000 BCE (5 months after GG)

Sullen and fatigued, the company of three made their return journey. It had been a month since they had left the Singing Mount. A sense of defeat hung in their hearts. Lunaya could not stop turning the events in her head. Perhaps if they had done something different... there was one thing that had been bothering her.

"Why would Maob care about Taivyn. What could he want with a young boy?" Lunaya finally asked.

Vayu stared at her in disbelief. He looked to Telzar, who stared blankly. "I've been wondering the same thing," Telzar said.

Have they never wondered about the boy's origin? Vayu had only now realized that neither of them knew. The faery elder looked around as if his surroundings would advise him on this matter. The Foothills of Alexandria were delicate compared to the magnitude of the mountain they had just scaled. The wind blew a little lighter in these parts. He listened to it as it moved through the stark, thin aspens – the only trees in this place. Conflicted between secrecy and truth, Vayu struggled with whether or not to divulge that which had been hidden. Finally, truth won.

Vayu explained to his human friends that just over sixteen years ago the faeries sent a little baby to the Moon Clan to be cared for and reared. Well, of course, Lunaya and Telzar had known that. There was no surprise there. They had all figured the faeries had discovered the baby abandoned. Unfortunately it happened once in a while. Humans were not immune to sickness and death. The parents could have died leaving the infant orphaned.

"Yes, we are fully aware of that, Vayu," Lunaya said. "I don't see what difference it makes."

"Let me assure you, it makes a great difference," Vayu replied. He looked around again as if to assure himself that he was doing the right thing. The winds blew and that comforted him. He sighed. Eventually this would all come to light sooner or later. Now was as good a time as any.

Vayu continued, "Almost seventeen years ago the Council swore an oath to protect a baby boy. They agreed to protect him because he was very special."

Vayu looked up at the sky. A few birds flew overhead. Their migratory pattern spoke to him. He knew the time had come. "That baby boy…the boy who you know as Taivyn…he is the last…."

Just then the birds flying overhead let out loud screeches as if the cacophony was an emphatic preamble to Vayu's final sentence: "He is the last member of the Dragon Clan."

Lunaya was stunned into silence. The look of shock on her face revealed that she had no idea. Lunaya was over one hundred years old. She hadn't seen a member of the Dragon Clan in at least half of that time, maybe longer. Telzar was silent as well. His face, however, was not readable. If he had been surprised by the revelation he had not shown it.

Finally Telzar asked, "So who knew about this?"

"Very few," Vayu assured. "Only the Council of Five and the Gnome King." Vayu paused. Then he continued reluctantly, "And the mother. The boy's mother knew."

****

Vayu explained that Elysinia had at first presumed the boy's mother to be dead – dispersed by the wind. However, she had not died. Having drunk from the Well of Knowledge, the boy's mother had lost her gift of longevity. She began to age rapidly, and for that reason, she had originally been unrecognizable to Elysinia.

Longevity was not the only thing she lost, though. Most importantly, and probably quite unbearably, she had also begun to lose her ability to dream with the dragons. Their spirit began to withdraw from her blood. It was that final evacuation of the dragon spirit from the boy's mother that Elysinia had witnessed, and which she had perceived as death.

It wasn't long after that the boy's mother returned, wanting to ensure that he was safe. Elysinia had assured her that he was. Apparently one of the mother's relatives had returned asking her questions.

"Another Dragon Clan member?" Telzar asked.

"No," Vayu said very clearly. "Not another Dragon Clan member. This one had not been chosen."

"Chosen?" Lunaya asked. Then recalling the ancient ways of that people: "Oh…you mean to say the dragons did not choose this person during the Dreaming Ceremony."

"I do. Yes," Vayu answered.

They walked on in silence for a while, all of them pondering in their own way. Several more weeks had passed and the terrain had shifted again. The Foothills of Alexandria ended at Mirror Lake – a dazzling body of water that reflected one's soul. The raft they had used on the way over was nowhere to be found. It would add several weeks to their journey to go around. Vayu listened to the winds. The clouds moved purposefully across the sky. The signs were clear. The Crossing of the Frog and the Mushroom was fast approaching. The conjunction would occur in a matter of weeks.

Lunaya understood the signs as well. "We have to make it back to the others before the Crossing. We have to tell them what we've discovered."

Vayu knew he could travel on the light and be there in no time. He could not transport his companions that way, however. And he would not leave them. It was not safe, not until they made it to the other side of the lake.

"Perhaps you should travel the light, Vayu," Telzar suggested as if reading Vayu's thoughts.

"Not an option," was Vayu's curt reply.

****

A black dot appeared over the horizon. It drew all of their attention. For a second they wondered what thing might it be. Then without a doubt they knew.

The black dot grew bigger and more pronounced. Then it began to circle. As it got closer they could make out the silhouette of feathered wings.

"Greetings Keeper. How lovely to see you. You are returning from your mountain journey, I presume."

"Yes," was the Keeper's reply. "Yuri, I need your help. It is imperative you get word to my brother and Elysinia. Would you deliver a message for me?"

Chapter 40
Taivyn and the Stone

"The philosopher should be a man willing to listen to every suggestion but determined to judge for himself. He should not be biased by appearances; have no favourite hypothesis; be of no school; and in doctrine have no master. Truth should be his primary object. If to these qualities he adds industry he may hope indeed to walk within the veil of the Temple of Nature."

- Michael Faraday

The Forest – 11,000 BCE (5 months after GG)

Groups of people were watching the Earth. Others seemed suspended in a dream state. There were dragon images, too. The dreaming ones seemed to be communicating with the dragons. The dragons rose up from the Earth's center. Flying, swimming, circling. They moved along the dragon lines of the Earth. The signs for the ages started to roll by – like a procession of symbols. A dragon flew by each one. The dragons awakened to turn the Wheel of the Ages: Earth, Air, Fire or Water. Finally a Silver Dragon rose high up in the sky, high above all the rest. There was one who stood on the Earth seeming to beckon to this magnificent Silver Being.

T aivyn stepped gently through the Forest trying not to upset the plants and creeping things that occupied the Forest floor. Unsettled and restless as a result of everything he'd been through, his nights remained rather sleepless. Not that the dreams were any help. Only now they came even when he was awake. This morning had brought him the most intense and comprehensive one yet.

Two days had passed since Taivyn left Amelda's cottage. Of course he had left that gnome behind. The gnome argued against it. He went on about the dangers. Well, Taivyn was sick of hearing about dangers. Besides, he knew where to find him if he felt so inclined. The gnome had gone over the meeting place a hundred times. Gnomes really were known for their redundancy.

After the dream this morning he had made the most unthinkable and possibly the rashest decision yet – he was going to return to the Moon Clan community. He wasn't going back for good but he needed help and he didn't know anywhere else to look for it. He needed to let go of the idea that returning to the community meant failure of his quest. He needed to remind himself that in fact this was all part of the quest. He kicked a stone in frustration.

Ouch!

"Ouch? Who said that?"

Taivyn looked down. The voice was coming from a small stone that lay nearly concealed by the blades of grass. It gave off a soft green and gold light that blinked dimly. Smooth on one side, while rough and jagged on the other, the tiny piece of stone appeared to be broken.

Chapter 41
Good To See You

"The physical universe is nothing other than the Self curving back within Itself to experience Itself as spirit, mind, and physical matter."

-Deepak Chopra, *The Seven Spiritual Laws of Success*

Moon Clan Community - 11,000 BCE
(5 months after GG)

Taivyn snuck inside the community boundaries, which was pretty easy, considering they didn't have any walls. They believed that defense provoked aggression. Well, they might very well have something to protect themselves from now if all this talk about danger was any indication.

Taivyn was a little nervous about seeing Korin. He didn't really know what to say or where to start. He wasn't sure how he was going to convince him that it was more important to listen to what he had to say than it was to reprimand him at this time. The days of being castigated were over. He was almost a man, and besides, he wasn't returning to the community for good – just long enough for him to get some help and possibly even find out more about this prophecy. Hopefully Korin would be that helping hand. He was counting on it. There were some other elders around, but believe it or not, Korin was his best bet, and Taivyn knew it.

He crept through the underground tunnels and caverns that ran beneath the Great Hall. Based on the day and time, if his guess was correct, Taivyn was sure that Korin would be just about finished with the middle kids now. Ages ten through twelve, they were Korin's favorite group to teach. They were old enough to reason with and yet they were young enough to not be limited in their thinking and imagination. Korin was usually in a fairly good disposition after this particular group. Taivyn was hoping to find him as such today.

Taivyn waited in the tunnel just below the Great Hall. Korin usually used this tunnel because he liked to avoid crowds and unsolicited conversation. What could one say? Korin was a no-nonsense kind of guy. Taivyn waited about fifteen minutes and began to think he might have goofed on the schedule because Korin should've been there by now. Taivyn really didn't want to show his face in a crowded space. The last thing he needed was to be recognized by anyone. It was safer that way; these days Taivyn was taking just a few more precautions than usual. After all, there was really no way of telling who, if anyone, knew what was going on. Better safe than sorry.

Just as he was about to retreat back into one of the stables, Taivyn saw a short, stocky figure coming through the tunnel. The figure stopped briefly, long enough for the glint of the torch to illuminate his reddish brown hair. It was Korin. Had he spotted Taivyn already? Damn, that guy was good. Taivyn couldn't get away with anything. He never could. The figure approached carefully and then rushed full on. What the hell? Taivyn started to make a beeline for the exit through the tunnel on the other side. Korin must have realized who it was because he stopped rushing him and called out.

"Taivyn? Is that you?"

Taivyn stopped before exiting. He turned to see Korin's features come into view. Korin got a little closer. "Holy Skies and Earth! Taivyn! What are you doing here? I thought you were gone for good."

"Well, I'm not back for good. You can be sure about that. But I'm back for now. And I need your help. Seriously. I'm feeling pretty lost and confused right now. And I might be in trouble."

"What else is new?" Korin rolled his eyes.

Immediately chiding himself for being so childish, Korin quickly adjusted his tone. "I'm sorry, Taivyn. I thought I might never see you again. Truth be told, I was kind of worried. And a little ashamed."

"Ashamed. Why? Why would you feel ashamed?"

"Because it was partly my fault that you left. If I had been a little easier on you and perhaps a little more understanding, then maybe you wouldn't have felt a need to run away."

"Korin, listen to me. It wasn't your fault. I needed to go. I may have been a little hasty, but ultimately I needed to learn about who I was."

"And have you?" Korin asked, genuinely interested.

"Well, yes, and no. I feel like I'm on the edge, Korin. You know…but there are still a lot of questions that need answers. It seems like the more answers I discover, the more puzzles seem to arise. Which is why I need you now…something big is happening. And I think – hell, I know – I am a part of it. But I've been warned that I may be in danger. Korin, will you help me?"

"Taivyn, of course, I will help you. Whatever you need," Korin said. "So what is going on?"

Taivyn recalled how it all started by getting lost in the woods. Taivyn recounted to Korin everything that had happened since he had left the community – everything from the dark presence he had felt in the woods, to sitting around the campfire with Ra-Ma'at, the spider and the gnomes, learning about the Frog and the Mushroom. Taivyn told him about Amelda. He even told him about Jedda.

Korin waited a while before he said anything. He wanted to ponder the story Taivyn told and that which he did not. Korin knew Taivyn was holding back. He sensed it was from years of not trusting anyone. He didn't really know how to help him move beyond that fear of trusting someone. Korin had been just like him at one time in his life. It was then that he hadn't trusted anyone, not even the Master. Korin suspected it was something like this with Taivyn. He was frank with him:

"Taivyn, when you left I didn't notice you were gone immediately, but after I didn't see you for about a week I sent word to the Master. It took him some time to respond, but I finally received a reply back that you had followed him into the Forest, and to not expect you back. I heard nothing further."

"Korin, I…." Taivyn tried to explain. He felt bad. Korin stopped him short.

"Taivyn, let me finish. After the Great Gathering, the Master and Elysinia spoke at length about the impending situation ahead. He has returned several times to explain how we can be of support during the Crossing of the Frog and the Mushroom, but has said nothing more about you, and I don't think it's for lack of caring. Taivyn, I think he means to keep you safe. I would hate for that all to be in vain."

"But Korin, if I'm meant to play a part in all of this then I need to know what the hell is going on. Enough with the secrets. Since when did the Moon Clan keep secrets anyway?!" Taivyn was frustrated.

"Since the fate of mankind and the planet depended on it!" Korin said, somewhat excitedly. Then he softened: "Now then, you came here for my help. Let me help you."

Taivyn had never seen Korin more genuine than in this moment. That's how one knows who the people are that can be counted on – because when things get tough, they don't flee; no, they are right there, by one's side. Korin was offering his help, knowing that the stakes were most probably quite high. The road they were going down could lead to all sorts of danger, most of which could not be anticipated. They didn't have the slightest clue what they were really up against. Taivyn believed Korin really did want to help him. Being able to trust him suddenly was like lifting a huge weight off of his shoulders. Taivyn softened.

"I'm really glad you said that, Korin. I sure hope you are able...." Taivyn looked around to make sure their conversation would be private, "Do you remember how the Master refused to tell you about the prophecy? He told you to go find it and read up on it...." Taivyn was trying to jog Korin's memory. He knew the conversation had taken place months ago.

"Yes, of course. That was the reason you left in the first place," Korin recalled. "The Master knew full well that it didn't exist within the Tower." Taivyn thought about that ancient library of artifacts – the highest and furthest part of the community walls. Korin continued, "That's why Master Ra-Ma'at left. Of course it was to go to the Great Gathering, but it was also to locate that prophecy. It's in the Crystal Library, or at least it was."

Now he had Taivyn's ear. He asked the obvious question, "And where is it now?"

Korin wasn't sure. No one was. Apparently there were mixed stories.

"Korin, do you know what it says?"

"No, not exactly. I know it has to do with the dragons, but beyond that is anyone's guess."

"Korin, I've been having...." Taivyn stopped short. *No, I'm not going to tell him about the dreams. Not yet, anyway.* Taivyn quickly took the conversation in a different direction: "I think I may be in possession of something that could tell us more…only I can't read it. It's written in some form of strange runes."

Taivyn moved to reveal the scroll, but then hesitated.

"What's wrong?" Korin asked. The boy was definitely exhibiting signs of paranoia.

"Korin, I think it might be best if we look this over someplace else. Somewhere that we won't have a chance of being disturbed or…," Korin caught his drift.

"Well, you've certainly learned a thing or three out there in the big wide world, or should I say Forest. Hell, you probably learned more out there than you ever did sitting in here." They both laughed out loud.

"Taivyn. I have to tell you it sure is good to have you back. You challenged me, you know that. I realized after you were gone how good you were for me. In my own growth process that is. You pushed my buttons. And that's good. It's good because it makes you grow beyond yourself."

Taivyn smiled in response.

"All right, let's get down to business. Meet me in the old barn in thirty minutes. I'll bring a candle so we can see," assured Korin.

"Right!" Taivyn sprang forth excitedly. Perhaps he was finally going to catch a break! Then he heard his stomach growl. With all the commotion he couldn't remember the last time he'd eaten. Maybe those black berries in the Forest a day or two ago. He looked at Korin imploringly.

"Korin, would it be too much trouble to ask you to bring…"

Korin caught on quickly and answered before Taivyn could finish his sentence, "Of course! You must be starving. Of course I'll bring you some food. Sit tight and I'll be back soon. Would some bread, berries, cheese and salt fish do?" Korin asked with a wink. Taivyn shot back a smile. He was beaming. Food always lightened his mood. Somehow Korin seemed to know that.

Chapter 42
A Burning Disaster

"Grant, O God, Thy protection; and in protection, strength; And in strength, understanding; and in understanding, knowledge; And in knowledge, the knowledge of justice; and in the knowledge of justice, the love of it; And in that love, the love of all existences; and in the love of all existences, the love of God – God and all goodness."

- Ross Nichols, *The Universal Druid Prayer*

Moon Clan Community – 11,000 BCE
(5 months after GG)

Korin arrived promptly, even a little early. He knew Taivyn was as anxious as he to examine the document he had somehow procured. He also knew the kid was famished. Knowing Taivyn, he wouldn't have missed a meal unless he absolutely had been in a situation where there had been no other options.

Traipsing through the Forest feeling himself in danger might just have qualified.

Making sure no one was around, Korin slipped unseen into the barn and set his supplies on the floor. At first, he did not see Taivyn. That one had certainly learned well how to be covert. Even when he had been living in the community, Korin remembered, he would scuttle all over the place, from here to there, hiding in barns and stables. He used to sneak out regularly in the evenings. No one had known except for Korin. Even back then Taivyn didn't completely trust anyone.

Of course this lack of trust never really made any sense to Korin. As far as he was concerned Taivyn was raised here. Having arrived as a baby, the only memories the boy had were of the Moon Clan Community. And no one had ever questioned his being there. At first others did wonder if he might be a halfling – part faery, part human. As time went on and he grew, they saw he was like everyone else.

At a young age, Taivyn had been informed about how he came to the community. The Moon Clan didn't believe in keeping secrets, even if it might have been for the best sometimes. Ever since Taivyn was informed about his arrival to the Moon Clan, he started questioning everyone including himself. Who could blame him? A child abandoned by not one, but two parents.

As Korin lit the wick of the candle, the whole space illuminated. He walked over to where the horses were situated and unsurprisingly found Taivyn there with them. He was nestled in a bed of straw on the ground next to Goldie. Goldie had always been Taivyn's favorite horse. He loved them all, however. Something drew the boy to the horses. Taivyn used to say he could understand them. Korin didn't know exactly what he meant, but in some way he could appreciate the boy's affection for the creatures. They were noble beings.

Taivyn was lying in the corner with his arm draped over Goldie. He must have been stroking her mane when he fell fast asleep. Korin thought it best to let the boy rest. Who knew how long it'd been since he had gotten a good night's sleep. He threw a blanket over the boy to keep him warm. Korin had brought it, assuming they would sit together and break bread on the ground.

He knew Taivyn might stir at some point, and he didn't want to leave him alone. He'd been alone enough. It was time he had some company. Korin propped his back up against the wood beams of the wall and settled in. He looked at the candle and wondered if he should blow it out. For safety reasons and because Korin was always thinking about safety precautions, he squelched the little flame between his fingers. The two of them lay sleeping in the barn with the horses. They slept peacefully through the night until just before first light.

****

Screams of chaos flooded the air. The shrill voices cut through their slumber like knives. Korin and Taivyn awoke terror-stricken. Immediately they could smell smoke. They jumped to their feet and looked around.

Without added light, they could hardly make out anything in the barn. They looked at each other for answers but there were none. Then they realized the pandemonium was coming from outside. Younger voices were screaming, "Fire! Fire!"

Taivyn and Korin scrambled outside. They came around the other side of the barn and beheld the sight in horror. Complete chaos was the scene. People were running frantically. The main building of the community dwelling was in flames. Some of the leaders were bringing water from the well in an effort to quell the flames.

Korin jumped into action with Taivyn by his side. "Taivyn, take my hands! When two or more are gathered…." Joining hands they closed their eyes. Korin connected his heart with the heart of Gaia. Tiny gnomes emerged from deep in the Earth; wispy sylphs swished through the air; water sprites gathered encased within minuscule droplets; fire spirits sparked and fizzled – tiny elemental beings of earth, air, water and fire began to gather in droves. *Harmony*, Korin thought. Then he said it aloud, "Harmony." Taivyn joined in the chant. Several more joined the circle with their voices and hearts. With love, honor and respect they continued chanting the simple but powerful word "harmony."

Suddenly the skies opened up. Water poured forth from the heavens. The flames flickered and sizzled before fizzling out. A perfectly contained rainstorm emerged out of nowhere – but it wasn't from nowhere. They knew it was their co-creative efforts with nature that allowed for this great blessing.

Only smoke remained where once a blazing conflagration had raged. The walls and siding were scorched, some beyond repair. Korin moved to quickly scan the scene. He was hoping everyone had made it out safely.

Jonah, one of the first elders to join their healing circle, was now walking the grounds assessing the damage. Lomi was catering to the children, offering consolation, while Kata was picking up some debris. This was their whole life, singed to ashes. Korin wondered about the Tower, and if any of the age-old scrolls and manuscripts had survived. He couldn't tell from where he was what shape the Tower was in. He was confused and angry. Taivyn looked distraught.

"What happened?" Taivyn whispered, his voice filled with disbelief and anguish.

"I don't know. It doesn't feel like an accident. I don't think it's a coincidence that the day after you arrived a fire breaks out."

"Korin, you don't think I had anything to do with this, do you?!" Taivyn asked in disbelief. He was shocked and hurt.

Korin quickly explained, "No, of course not. I know you were in here with me. And I know your heart. I know you'd never do anything like this."

Korin caught his breath. The initial shock abating, the devastation was just now sinking in. "What I mean is that I think it's all connected. Let me run over and speak with Jonah." Jonah and Korin were peers, but saw to very different job duties. Where Korin instructed the younger initiates, Jonah was a master healer. Herbs, stones and Earth Light were only a few of the skillful modalities in which he was adept.

Korin considered asking Taivyn to stay behind but thought better of it. Taivyn's presence had now clearly been revealed. Besides, trying to keep the kid out of things turned out to be an error on their part. He would not repeat the mistake twice. Before Korin could speak, Taivyn pleaded.

"Korin, please let me help in any way I can. I don't want to be left out. Not now. I need to be able to help my people."

Korin was taken by surprise. For the first time in his life Taivyn was identifying with the community as his own. He wouldn't deny Taivyn's request to help. Not now. Korin nodded his ascent for Taivyn to join him. They both jogged over to where Jonah was investigating one of the fallen beams. The light of the sun caused his tears to look like glistening streams upon the dark skin of his face.

"I didn't expect to see you, Taivyn. Korin, where were you when all this started? We couldn't find you anywhere."

Korin apologized for not being there for everyone. Taivyn could see how torn Korin was. He knew he was happy to have been able to take care of Taivyn, and yet he also felt like he'd let everyone down by not being there. Jonah assured him he had nothing to be upset about. He was in his right and perfect place in the right and perfect time. What was important was that they could come together now as a community.

"Yes, we must come together. To rebuild and…." Korin started to speak about being strong in the face of adversity when Jonah interrupted gently, as was his way.

"Rebuild yes, but first there are more important things. We must understand why the attack came."

"Attack?" Korin and Taivyn said simultaneously.

"Yes, this fire was started by a band of marauders. We all thought they were a bunch of brutes looking to pillage food and provisions. We offered them whatever they wanted if they'd leave us unharmed."

Korin swallowed hard. "And did they leave you unharmed?" He hoped like hell they had.

"Yes, but they threatened that if they returned we wouldn't be so lucky," Jonah confirmed. Korin and Taivyn both relaxed a little. Material things could always be fixed or replaced. Lives lost could not.

"So what did they end up taking?"

"Not much. They searched high and low. They went to the Tower. Some things were taken from there. The rest was set afire."

Korin cringed as the pit of his stomach tightened. All the Wisdom of the Ages, countless volumes of ancient wisdom. Gone. He couldn't fathom it. It was too much. He thought of the Master then, and how devastating a blow this would be to him. He would be shattered.

Jonah continued, "I don't know what they were looking for but I got the idea it wasn't an 'it'. I got the impression they were searching for someone."

Taivyn flushed with shame and embarrassment. He managed, "What made you think that?"

"Well, as they were searching and tearing everything apart the one who seemed to be the leader – he wore a mask and the others appeared to take orders from him – kept yelling, 'Find him! Find him! Leave no stone unturned!'"

Crushed and dejected, Taivyn confessed, "Oh no. This is all my fault. They were looking for me. I just know it."

"Son, this is no one's fault. This is the doing of misguided men. Not you. It doesn't matter who they were looking for. And I am glad they didn't find them. I don't know what they planned, but I shouldn't wish for anyone to fall victim to their twisted plot."

Korin thought about everything and wondered aloud, "Were they just random marauders, or did you recognize any of them?"

"Funny you should ask. At first I thought the attack was random, and that it was just a group looking for one of their own that might have fled, or what have you. Right before they left the leader addressed me…by name! It was then that I realized I recognized his voice."

Korin and Taivyn waited silently for Jonah to elaborate. They both had a sick feeling inside. Neither, however, was expecting what he said next.

"It was Maob."

Chapter 43
A Prophecy Revealed

"It tells of the sacred letters, the Ogam – but more I will not say, for it is a mystery. Yet, for those able to see, there is a deeper lesson to learn and a key to one of the secrets of the Wood, where each kind of tree is a key to a lock that only the Cauldron-born may unlock, after long and difficult trials."

-John Matthews, *The Song of Taliesin*

Moon Clan Community –11,000 BCE
(5 months after GG)

K orin and Taivyn rushed back to the barn. Now more than ever, the boy had to know what the scroll revealed. Time was of the essence, and he felt it foolish to not know what he was going up against. A plan would have to be devised.

Korin broke out the little basket that held the food, while Taivyn produced the scroll. They walked over to the right wall where several windows let the sunlight pour in. They weren't hungry. After everything that had happened, the last thing they could think about was eating. And yet they knew they must keep up their strength for what was most surely ahead. Taivyn stuffed a few bread crusts in his mouth and washed it down with a swig of water from the clay pitcher that Korin had carried over. Korin munched on some berries and took a couple pieces of cheese.

Taivyn took out the scroll from its protective sheath and unfurled it on the ground carefully as to not damage the document. They positioned it so the sunlight hit it in just the right way, illuminating it perfectly so they were able to see.

Taivyn was curious: "So do you think you can read it, Korin?"

Korin examined the scroll, carefully scrutinizing each and every detail. The document appeared ancient. Its edges were worn and slightly frayed. What seemed to be a large watermark stained the corner. Luckily this did not obscure any of the writing.

"Taivyn…." The boy lifted his head.

"Based on the images next to the script, I think this may be the prophecy…."

"The prophecy? I thought the prophecy was inside a crystal?"

"Well, yes. But I'm not talking about the original. I think this is a copy. It seems to be a transcription of sorts…."

Taivyn couldn't believe his good luck. Could it be after all this time that the actual prophecy that spoke about him had been lying right under his nose and he didn't even know it?

Korin lifted it to examine the backside of the document. There was no writing there, only on the one side. Korin held up a tiny glass instrument to his eye. Used to magnify things on a page, it was small and roundish. He scanned from one side to the other, right to left, up and down, then down and up. He was looking for something. Taivyn knew this sort of thing required patience and precision, but he was on pins and needles. He couldn't take the anticipation.

"Korin, you're not saying anything! Can you read it or not?" he blurted, unable to control himself.

"Well, yes and no. I think I might be able to, but…."

"But what?" Did Korin realize he was practically killing him with suspense?

"Well, was there anything else with the scroll?" Korin asked.

"What do you mean?"

"I'm not sure. You see, I think this is a transcription of Elyrie. However, the language is so much more than writing on a page. There would usually be a key in the document that would illuminate that which was unseen to most…."

"A key?" Taivyn didn't understand.

"Yes, somewhere on the document itself, or maybe it would have been separate, but kept near to it."

Disappointment crept from around the corner and stared at Taivyn. He had been so close. Who knew in all those parchments and papers what, if anything, might have been a so-called key.

"I don't know, Korin. I mean if there was, I didn't see it. There were so many scrolls, I wouldn't have known which one...."

Korin interrupted him, "No, it probably wouldn't have been in the form of a scroll."

"Well, how do you know? You were looking for it on this scroll."

"Yes, but not in the way you think. Elyrie is the song of all songs. Things written in Elyrie aren't what they seem."

"Elyrie is the language of the faeries, right? Oh, oh and the trees!" Taivyn was proud of himself for having remembered something of his classes.

"Yes, but it is not just *their* language; it is the language of Gaia herself. It's more than a tool for communication. Elyrie is like a portal that takes you into yourself. It's a transmission of the Mysteries of the Universe to one's soul."

"So shouldn't everyone be able to read it, then?"

"It is written that long ago, everyone could. Now, however, many have to be trained in this wisdom to activate the memory that lies deep within."

"But haven't you been trained, Korin?"

"Yes, to some extent. But this transmission isn't complete. It's missing the key. Without the key, it's just a bunch of symbols. The key makes them come alive...."

"So what would the key have looked like if not a scroll?"

"I don't know. A crystal maybe...or...," Korin racked his brain for some other example, "Well, it doesn't matter anyway, I guess. Not unless you want to go back there. You would have known if you...."

"That's it! Maybe I did grab something else!" Taivyn rushed over to where his bundle lay. Diving in like a kid into a swimming hole, he emptied everything out. Among the items that fell out was a small pouch. Grabbing it, he jumped back over to where Korin waited. Taivyn reached his hand inside to produce three stones with markings on them – the stones he'd gathered up off the table at Amelda's when he was tidying the cottage. Korin's eyes lit up. The boy just may have done it.

"Taivyn, these stones could be it."

Korin held out his hand. Taivyn offered them freely. He placed them at various points on the scroll. Suddenly, the stones flashed. Like little portals to another world, they turned translucent and light-filled. Three colored rays poured out, one from each stone, where they met in the middle to form a cone of soft purple light. Then the document became illuminated. The symbols were alive. They danced and whirled on the scroll. Then a song descended from the sky and rose from the depths of the Earth. It opened their hearts to be able to see.

> *The clan who have in their veins,*
> *The wisdom of the dragon ways,*
> *Have the power to dream and call,*
> *The dragons for the good of all.*

But the Silver One of royal make,
Earth, air, fire, water - all only he can awake.
Every Age when he walks the earth,
All the dragons rejoice in mirth.
At age sixteen his memories flow,
Up from the dragon dreams below.
After the Turn, his body should it need rest,
To the Inner Earth he joins the nest.
If ever his soul should come to sleep,
On the Earth a darkness so deep.
The only salvation against his foes,
The union of the Dragon and the Rose.

The words were so familiar, like a bedtime story he'd been told over and over again. Only he'd never been told any of it, not in the way one would expect. He was transported to his dreams and visions. He could feel the dragons' movements in his heart. It was a connection so deep, he had been terrified to let it in, to surrender to it. There was no rational reason for the affection he felt for these creatures. It was as if he'd known them always, like they were his childhood friends. He loved these creatures like he loved the horses, like he loved...Jedda. He thought of her, and he thought of the Rose. The pieces started falling into place.

"Korin, I think there are people who work with dragons. I think that's what this is talking about... Korin, I think that's what Maob's looking for.

"The Dragon Clan?"

"Yes. You see, I've been having these dreams. I think these are my people. I mean, Korin, I know what they teach us in class, but did you really believe there were dragons?"

"Well, yes, it's something that we all learn about, but no one ever talks about them beyond that. And they only ever come anymore at the...."

"At the what? At the what, Korin?!"

"At the Turning of the Ages...."

"Of course...," Taivyn trailed off. He recalled his latest dreams. A dispirited wretchedness crept in, and his face turned sour. Reflected in his eyes was panic.

"Korin, Maob wants to control the dragons."

"That's silly. No one can. Other than maybe these people, the Dragon Clan. But they don't control them; it's a relationship. Maob must know that. I don't think we have anything to worry about."

"You're wrong, Korin. I think he wants to use the power from the Crossing of the Frog and the Mushroom to control the dragons!"

Korin's eyes grew wide with apprehension. "Holy Moon and Stars!"

"Korin, I have to go into the Forest. I have to find the Frog and the Mushroom."

"Well, that's ridiculous. You'll walk right into his hands. If he's looking for you, why make it so easy?"

"I need to try and stop him."

"Well, then I'm coming with you."

"No, Korin. The community needs you here. Someone has to help them rebuild. Besides what if Maob comes back? They'll need you."

"You're not going alone."

"I won't. I know someone who will help me. I just need to get to him." Taivyn thought of Gorlin who had insisted over and over he was making a mistake by not taking his help.

"You are going to need me," Gorlin had told him, "Wait, you will see."

Chapter 44
A Lonely Traveler

"He [Carl Jung] was to call them
[plants and trees] 'thoughts of God,' expressing not
only the mind of the creator but also the magnetic
beauty of the instant of creation."

– Laurens Van Der Post,
Jung and The Story of Our Times

The Forest – 11,000 BCE (5 months after GG)

U nsure of his next move, he slowly emerged from underneath a luscious green leaf. Only a delicate dewdrop was shaken from its place of stillness as it splashed upon the plush top of the small being. Like a light misty shower upon its white speckled red head (if indeed a head it could even be called), the mushroom felt refreshed after his lengthy and very calculated patience.

A tune, liquid and lulling, was traveling through the trees. Like wild wind chimes and harp strings, this song, while heard by many, was for the mushroom alone. He longingly listened to the intoxicating lilt as he glided across streams and over tree roots. He had come close to crossing paths with the song's source several times before, but he had known the time had not been right.

He was also aware of those who traced his movements, and yet he did not move or delay because of them. Nay, that would have been foolish to choose a movement out of fear. A being such as he would never allow his choices to be dictated by external factors. For it is known that true power can only come from within.

The mushroom was neither a creature of good nor evil. He was one who just simply was. He lived for the sheer enjoyment of existence. And while he lived in this world mostly, he was not of it. His road was a lonely one because he was unlike most any other creature in the Forest. And yet there was one who understood him well – one who knew him and honored him for who and what he was. And while this one admired the pristine power that made up each of the mushroom's movements, he did not desire that power for himself. And it was this one whose song the mushroom heard now.

The mushroom himself was not a powerful being. No. The mushroom had only ever been dedicated to living impeccably. It was in this impeccability that the power lay. He did not choose to use it or direct it in any way. He simply wanted to be left alone to live and enjoy his nearly immortal life. Besides, it was only ever in the moment of his crossing paths with the one who understood him that this power could be recognized and used for darkness or for light.

Just then the frog's song sounded a chord that struck deep within the mushroom's core. He made a decisive motion and scurried without moving across the Forest floor and into a cornucopia of weeds and things that go bump in the night. Lost once again to the naked eye, the mushroom continued on his journey.

Chapter 45
A Tryst with a Tree

"As the BBC documentary Planet Earth succinctly said of our biological relationship to trees, 'If they didn't live here, neither would we.'"

-Jean Shinoda Bolen, *Like a Tree*

The Forest – 11,000 BCE (5 months after GG)

The Great Oak stood tall and proud. Its branches hung low with the weight of the wind that pressed against it as it thrashed about. Looking around with a bird's-eye view, the raven had made his perch, as always, on the highest branch. A shadow moved in the night. A shadow that was both light and dark. Purple light streamed through here and there and colored the bird's feathers, giving them a sheen that was iridescent against the moonlight.

Through the circle of standing trees, the purple light grew near. Then it flickered and expanded into a shaded bubble. Two figures appeared inside. Like clear glass, the bubble reflected hues of blue and violet and silver. The bubble dissipated and only the two remained.

"I am so glad that I was able to accompany you to speak with the Old One this night. Rose, I will miss you so! This may be our last time we travel the light together."

"Don't say that, Guinevere. Never say that. Besides we don't know what it will be like. Perhaps we may still travel the light when we have crossed."

Guinevere was a younger faery of exquisite beauty. Whispers of pink fire light graced the wispy silver locks on her delicate head. Upon her form she wore a satin garment of dazzling blue peppered with tiny sapphire and emerald jewels that sparked and flared when she spoke. Golden ringlets decorated her arms as if they were sunlit vines that grew from her skin.

"But *they* don't travel the light. They aren't able." Guinevere reminded her companion.

"Gwen, we both don't have to go. None of you do. Only one. And I...I have agreed to do this."

"Rose, you do not have to bear this burden alone. And don't forget – I wanted to go! I have always wanted to go. It has not been presented until now."

Rose nodded. She knew Gwen wouldn't change her mind, for it had been her greatest desire to explore the realm of humans for herself. It might not be all glamour and light, though. Rose let it go. Who was she to decide another's path? Then she remembered her friend's situation.

"Gwen, how silly of me not to have asked. How is Leori doing with all this, anyway?"

"He's proud...and sad. He will miss me and I him. Especially now that Mother is gone."

As a member of the Council of Five, Leori had chosen to remain in the Forest, while Leona, his mate, had already entered deep into the Mists. His daughter, Gwen, was all he had left. Rose felt sad for Leori. She empathized deeply, for she knew what it was to be separated from your beloved.

"But he will see Leona again...," Rose said, but it was more of a reassurance for herself than anything else.

"Yes. He will...." Gwen was pensive, "I suppose, in a sense, we all will see one another again."

Rose approached the tree. Just moving into his great presence soothed her whole being. She glided closer and reached out for him. Then she sat gently down with her back to his trunk. Closing her eyes, she began to breathe with the tree. Gwen stood watching. What a great gift the Faery People had been given – the Language of the Trees. Tiny crystal lights flowed within the tree's trunk. Streams of ultra-violet moved up and through its branches, pulsing awareness into the atmosphere. The tree was life. The trees meant life. How much life's journey resembled that of a tree.

The rivulets of gold came pouring into Rose, like a royal dance being performed. The joy shone on Rose's face. Her body laughed and smiled. The golden light grew around her, and poured into her. Through the language of the soul, the Great Oak spoke to her. He spoke to her of what was and what would be. Rose's expression changed from joy to sadness to sheer bliss and then to despair.

"The Keepers will forget?" she questioned as she got up from where she'd nestled.

The tree glowed green and golden. Streams of images came into her heart. A greater understanding occurred.

"I understand. Yes. The cycles. I must remember even when I am...."

"Human." Gwen finished her sentence. Rose had not yet owned it.

"Yes. Even then. The Moon Clan will forget – even the Keepers. They will lose their ability to hold the Language of the Trees within their bodies."

Rose had known that possibility was the reason she attempted the crossover in the first place. She hadn't actually seen the truth of it, however. Now she did.

She tried to reassure herself, "After all, it's only 13,000 years until the next 'light' part of the cycle...."

Rose didn't realize then that time affected faeries very differently than it did humans. And so she didn't really understand what that meant. She didn't understand death the way humans knew it, either. What she really had no way to know or understand was that she would live and die thousands of times, mostly forgetting who and what she was.

"Rose, our immortality will be lost," said Gwen.

"Right," responded Rose.

But she wasn't so sure. It seemed quite the same. Humans were immortal, too. They just didn't have the continuity, it seemed. They went through the death process, but just like everything in nature, they were always reborn. The tree continued its dialogue:

Crystal images and silver light. A Serpent whose tail was long, long like the Earth, rode through the realms on waves of vibration. Serpentine waves emanated from its body. The tail wrapped itself around the Mother with a love so tender. Its rhythmic undulations indicated its sleep and dream patterns. Then with a flutter, its eyes opened. The eyelids vibrated and lifted slowly. The Rose could be seen being grasped at its feet.

Rose screamed, "No! He's here. He's been here. How could it be? I would have known. I would have felt or seen or heard something!"

Rose fell to the ground, gasping for air or life force or something. Had he been here and not come for her? There must be some misunderstanding.

"Tarin…," the name escaped her lips with longing and desire – a love so deep and true. It was a love like no other.

Gwen bent down to help the faery up. "Rose, are you okay, my sweet friend? What have you been shown?"

She thought of Tarin. Only his name wasn't Tarin now. Of course Elysinia would have ensured he were named something else to keep him obscured – even from her. If only she had known he'd come back. Why hadn't her mother told her?

"Come, Rose. We should get back. To the festivities."

Rose answered sullenly, "Yes…."

The faeries looked lovingly upon the Great Oak. Their gaze moved from one tree to another in the perfect circle.

"I can't imagine I would ever exist where trees were not," Rose said.

"Don't be silly, Rose. I don't think there are such places!" Gwen laughed at Rose's imagination.

Chapter 46
The Rose

"As a hunter examines the grass for the track of the deer, as a love looks for response in the face of the beloved, so we, too, need to search the hinterland of that further shore with imagination and intelligence."

- Caitlin Matthews, *Celtic Visions*

The Forest – 11,000 BCE (6 months after GG)

The gnome had been waiting exactly where he said he'd be. Who knew how long the gnome had been standing in that spot? It seemed to Taivyn when he arrived like he had been waiting casually for a short while, and yet that would have been impossible. How would the gnome have known when or if Taivyn would arrive?

"Have you been here the whole time?" Taivyn demanded.

A cryptic answer was all Taivyn got: "Here, there. It matters not. One place is as good as another. And really, from below, they are all pretty much the same."

Taivyn sighed. "Well, how did you know I would come?"

"I told you that you were going to need me."

Taivyn and Gorlin had been traveling nearly a week since then. Gorlin watched the sky every night. He read the messages written in the stars above. He understood silent words spoken by the stones on the ground. Every now and then they would stop and listen to a bird as it sang its song. The song told of many things, but most of all, it spoke of one – the Frog and the Mushroom would cross at any moment.

Taivyn reminded Gorlin of Amelda. Perhaps that was what caused the gnome to ask after a week of walking together: "Do you miss Amelda?" They hadn't spoken much the entire journey. Apparently Gorlin wasn't much of a conversationalist. Practical and very to the point, the gnome seemed a stranger to idle discussion.

The question had caught Taivyn off guard. He hadn't expected Gorlin to speak at all, but a question about Amelda really knocked Taivyn on the head. After the initial shock, Taivyn thought about the question. Of course, he missed her. She was the closest thing to a mother that he had ever experienced. No one ever doted on him the way she did. He figured it was because he had saved her life. Now he realized there may have been more to it than that. Taivyn was starting to believe in Fate. Perhaps it was Fate that had allowed his path to cross with hers.

"I do miss her, Gorlin. I just felt connected to her in some way – like we were family. I hadn't been there with her for very long, but still...I believe we had a bond."

The gnome studied Taivyn very closely, squinting as if he were trying to read the boy. Gorlin raised his eyebrows suspiciously.

Gorlin said, "You don't know, do you?"

"Know what?" Taivyn asked.

At that moment a stream of smoke that cut through the trees caught their attention. They rushed toward the direction from which the smoke blew and discovered a lively group in celebration and joy. There were faeries and humans among them and animals too. Many of the faery elders were present. So, too, were Astriel and Lir of the Moon Clan. Elysinia glimpsed Gorlin and Taivyn. This was unexpected. She thought of Rose.

"Taivyn, what are you doing here?" Lady Astriel asked, concerned and filled with compassion. If there was any punishment in her voice, he couldn't tell.

"Well, you certainly have got friends in high places," Lir said, looking at Gorlin.

"What is that supposed to mean?" Taivyn wanted to know.

"The Gnome King. He's not bringing you here because you got into trouble?" Lir winked. The rest laughed.

"The Gnome King...Gorlin?"

"On a first-name basis, too! This boy is really something." They all laughed again.

"I assure you, this is no laughing matter." It was Gorlin, and whatever merriment the gnomes were accustomed to displaying, there was none present. This one was as serious as a graveyard.

"I've come to warn you all!" Taivyn spoke up. "Lady Astriel, I need to speak with Master Ra-Ma'at. Please. I think we may be in danger."

"What is it, Taivyn? You shouldn't be here," Elysinia said as the crowd cleared, allowing her to speak.

"Lady Elysinia, I must speak with the Master. Where is he?"

Just as Taivyn started to explain everything, a figure of white light walked toward the group. She had materialized from the large mound that protruded from the ground near the meadow. Small footsteps left a trail of flowers as she approached. She was beautiful and familiar. Rusted hair with golden red strands glided and danced around her face. Twirling around her starlit skin was a dazzling green light-filled gown. *Jedda?* Taivyn wondered, surprised. *What is she doing here?* he thought.

****

As she stepped from beyond the folds, Rose saw someone standing near Gorlin that she thought she recognized. Her heart jumped. Tarin? So it's true. The young man had been talking to her mother animatedly about something when he noticed her. Rose walked up to where they were.

"Jedda!"

"I'm sorry. I don't know who that is, but…." Rose shot Elysinia a look colored with betrayal. Then Rose turned back to Taivyn: "How could it be? I thought you were gone. I thought you had…."

Taivyn was confused, but didn't really care. Without thinking he flung his arms around her, "Jedda, My Lady, I thought I'd never see you again!"

Rose continued staring at him in disbelief. Taivyn didn't know how to act. My God! To see her again! He had never expected it! Up close though, he noticed small differences about her. Her hair was longer and almost translucent. Light shined through it, or from within the strands. Her height, well, she was taller. Of course he didn't give much thought to that because women were sometimes known to wear interesting shoes that created this effect. The strangest thing was her skin. It sparkled like crystal light. Like the girl that had emerged from the mists while he had waited for Jedda at the circle of trees, this one was almost a spitting image of Jedda, and yet different. Who was she?

"I'm sorry. Who is Jedda?" Rose asked.

"I thought you were her. You look just like her…,"Taivyn said.

"My name is Rose. I am the daughter of Elysinia. I am Faery."

"Faery…Rose…?" Taivyn stammered. He felt the same electric waves moving through his fingertips as he had with Jedda. Her eyes sparkled like the bluest water he had ever seen. His heart was racing, and with each pulsing beat, bubbles popped inside his chest. Light was folding into itself and then unfolding and expanding within him.

"That's right." She smiled.

"Huh?" Taivyn was spinning.

Rose looked lovingly at him. She loved him with all her heart and soul – even if he did look slightly disheveled. She gazed at his soft aura that had always marked his presence. Then she saw something else…the silver scale…she glanced at his wrist. Nothing. But there in the inner layer of his energy field, something shined brightly and definitely silver. But who had hidden it there?

Elysinia interrupted. "Rose," she pleaded with her daughter, "you must understand."

"Mother, did you know he had returned? You knew all this time and did not tell me? How could you?"

"It has only been sixteen years, my Daughter. And I could not risk it. No one knew. Not even Ra-Ma'at, even though I had placed him within the Moon Clan community."

Rose felt angry that this wonderful part of her life had been kept secret. If only she'd known she could've spent her last remaining time with him, for who knew what would become of her?! Who knew if what they all hoped for would even work?! Emotions ravaged her, causing tears to well in her eyes.

Taivyn barely noticed anyone else. Staring at Rose, he was in a world all his own where only the two of them existed. Time stood still. He felt her tears as if they were his own. And while he didn't know why, it seemed like lifetimes of pain gnawed at him and begged him to be set free. At that moment Rose met his gaze. He looked deeply into her eyes. Lightning struck him from the inside out. All became wavy and unfocused. Taivyn was transported to another time.

A field of wildflowers. The two who sat in its center were really one. The one with starlit skin and sapphire eyes reached out her delicate hand. A rose she offered him now.

"So you will always remember. Take this. Its memory will be etched upon your heart and soul, and even while you sleep you will remember. Our love will always lead you back to me. No matter how many times you lay in rest, I will find you time and time again, until the two of us become one once again. I love you, My Sweet Prince.

"And I, you, My Beautiful Rose. I will remember."

Then Taivyn found himself amidst the circle of people he had left only moments ago. "Rose?"

"You remember." Rose smiled, "I knew you would come back to me, My Love."

He looked around at all the faces. Torches were lit, glowing balls of light that illuminated the Forest, like a Midsummer's Night. He noticed the festivities for the first time.

"It is I that must go away this time, My Love. But with the hard work of everyone here, and a little faith, I shall come out on the other side."

"Other side of what?" Taivyn didn't comprehend where she was going.

"Of the bridge, My Love. I am choosing to become mortal."

"Mortal?"

"Yes…when I appear on the other side then all will be as it should be. And how wonderful will it be that we will be able to spend at least one mortal life together!"

"What if you don't appear on the other side?"

Then Master Ra-Ma'at appeared, causing Taivyn to remember his reason for coming here in the first place. The boy became nervous and flustered. Not having seen the Master since he ran from him in the Forest made him feel rotten and ashamed.

"Taivyn, I cannot tell you how happy I am to see you right now. How wonderful that you are here! As if everything is working out in Divine Order. I suspect those universal laws won't change. Not even in the coming Age of Sleep."

"Yes, Master! That is why I am here! I have come to warn you. I think Maob is going to do something awful."

"Maob?" Ra-Ma'at was surprised to hear the name fall from the boy's mouth. A feeling of dread came over the Solar Keeper. He had always suspected, but….

Taivyn interrupted his thoughts: "The Moon Clan. Maob was at the community. He set it afire."

"For the love of the Forest! Was anyone hurt?" Ra-Ma'at eyes reflected deep concern. What was the boy telling him? Could it really be true?

"No, no one was hurt. But I think he was searching for me…." Taivyn felt this was all his fault somehow.

Worry and anxiety had tainted his cheerful mood. Ra-Ma'at felt deeply concerned for the boy. Why would Maob be searching for Taivyn? They had been so careful. Ra-Ma'at hadn't even confided in Korin what he had discovered. It didn't make any sense. Nevertheless, if what Taivyn said was true, and Maob was indeed looking for him, then…. "Taivyn, you mustn't be here," he said.

"But Master, he is going to try to summon the dragons, and…."

"Taivyn, listen to me, I understand why you did what you did. You had to. And I was wrong to keep things from you. I wanted to keep you safe, but I lost sight of one very important thing. You have every right to make choices for yourself. You aren't a boy anymore. You reminded me so much of myself when I was young that I just wanted to protect that innocence in you, in me. Now I realize I was wrong to do so. Please forgive me."

The Master was apologizing to him! Taivyn couldn't believe his ears. Really, this alone might be a once in a lifetime happening. He looked at the Master filled with love. He felt so much warmth coming from him. He knew the Master had meant every word of what he had just spoken. He gave the boy a warm bear hug that melted Taivyn's shame and embarrassment right away.

In that moment, Gorlin stepped forward. "He has the Prophecy Egg!"

287

Everyone gasped.

"Taivyn, I am so sorry, but your mother gave it to us for safekeeping. We have failed her. And you." The Gnome King was downcast. "We don't know how but we suspect…no matter. What's done, is done."

The bombshell had been dropped. Taivyn's head was swimming. His chest tightened. He felt suffocated like he was drowning and no matter what he did he could not breathe. Coming up to the surface for air was not an option because the surface no longer existed.

"My mother?" Taivyn heard himself ask. The question had come out of his own lips, but he couldn't hear himself. It was as if he were floating outside of himself, looking in.

"Yes, Taivyn," Elysinia finally said. "Amelda was your mother."

Chapter 47
A Man Apart

"If you would judge aright of human life, you must arise and stand upon the crest of time and note the thoughts and deeds of men as they have come up through the ages past."

- Levi Dowling,
The Aquarian Gospel of Jesus the Christ

The Forest – 11,000 BCE (6 months after GG)

A lone and rocking back and forth, he sat. His arms hugged his legs that were folded close to his chest. Tears slid down his cheeks. After a time, Ra-Ma'at walked over toward Taivyn and sat down beside him. He placed his arm around the boy. A tear slid down the Keeper's face. Ra-Ma'at could feel the boy's pain.

Without looking up at Ra-Ma'at, Taivyn asked, "Did you know? Did you know all this time?"

"I did not. I only just found out a short while ago." Elysinia had listened to the stories of the Forest. The trees had whispered news of the miraculous reunion.

Taivyn remembered Amelda's last words to him: "I'm sorry I have to leave you again...."

"So she had known the whole time?!" Taivyn wanted to know.

"She did not. Not until she drank from the Well of Knowledge." Word had spread through the Forest that this had been the case. Amelda had been beloved by all the Forest creatures, in particular the gnomes. The gnomes had a special affinity for Dragon Clan members, as they had a special affinity for the dragons. Amelda was kind and generous. When Ra-Ma'at had learned about it, he became deeply agitated, wondering what this would do to the boy.

"The well gave her 'sight,' but her youth was the price for such knowledge." Taivyn knew it was the well that had made her sick. He didn't know why anyone would be willing to trade their life for knowledge. What a waste!

"She did it for you, Taivyn! Don't you see that?" Ra-Ma'at had to make the boy see what his mother had really done. She had sacrificed herself for him, not once but twice. Her baby had been born with the Silver Scale. She knew of the ancient prophecy of their people. The Dragon Clan had dwindled considerably. At the age of eight hundred, her sister Aneta had died the year before. Only Amelda and her husband Gero still lived. Amelda grew worried. Her dreams made her uneasy. She feared for the safety of her son. Most of all, she feared for the safety of those she had sworn to protect. She would often sit with the Prophecy Egg, wondering if the foes it spoke of referred to the present time.

Finally, Amelda did the unthinkable. She had heard of the Well of Knowledge – a well whose water contained answers to any question that one had. Gero begged Amelda not to drink. They argued day and night. Finally, she prevailed. The Silver Prince would always be in danger because of the power he possessed. She had to know. So she drank. She drank to know what might come. She drank to understand what precautions she might take to ensure the survival of her people, of the dragons, and of her son.

"Why couldn't she teach me about the dragons?" Taivyn asked.

"Because it was the price of drinking from the well. She lost her ability to dream with the dragons and," Ra-Ma'at continued, "that wasn't the only thing she lost. She lost your father."

"My father...?" It felt so strange saying those words.

"Yes, Gero died shortly after she drank from the well. It happened after Amelda brought you to the faeries. He felt his wife was no longer the same. And you were gone. He died of heartbreak," Ra-Ma'at finished the story.

Taivyn felt like his insides were ripping out. Tears spilled down his face. He rubbed his wet cheeks with his arm.

"Well, why in the name of Great Spirit would she not recognize me?"

"Because I swore an oath to protect you," said Elysinia as she appeared from the trees.

****

Elysinia walked over then. When seated beside Taivyn, she waved her hand around Taivyn's head. Sparks of light fizzled in the air around him like a cloud electrically charged. "Hold out your wrist," she said. Then she waved her hand over it. There, on the inside of his arm, at the center of his wrist, was a tiny silver dragon scale.

"The mark of the Silver Prince," Ra-Ma'at gasped. To see the scale was a marvel.

"The natural ability of light is both to illuminate and conceal. I concealed your scale to veil your identity. My magic allowed me to shield you from any who would recognize your form." Elysinia continued, "As I said, I promised your mother I would keep you safe. I am sorry it kept you even from her, but it was necessary. I hope you understand."

Then the one he wanted to see most sat down beside him. He hadn't known until she was seated how incomplete he felt without her. Rose was a comforting balm to his tired soul. Ra-Ma'at and Elysinia took their leave, allowing the two soul mates to be alone.

"I am sorry you had to find out about your mother like that. I didn't know either," Rose said. She was beautiful. He had never seen anything like her. When she spoke his whole soul responded, like he was listening to himself. Never had he felt comfort and peace – until this very moment.

"Rose, I am so glad you are here."

"As am I, My Love." Her eyes shimmered in the light of the hanging baubles that glowed in the trees. The decorations were splendid designs of opulence and enchantment. If anyone knew how to put on a celebration, it was the High Faeries.

"So what about the Prophecy Egg and Maob…?" Taivyn wanted to know. Had everyone forgotten what was going on here?

"It doesn't matter. We have scouts everywhere. Regardless, he cannot control the dragons. No use of force will work. I don't know what he means to accomplish, but it's futile. Taivyn, you are the only one who can work with the dragons."

"Are you sure? But the power of the Crossing…."

Rose answered, "Not even with all the power of the Crossing. It won't work."

Then Elysinia and Ra-Ma'at returned. "Come!" said Ra-Ma'at to the both of them. "The Crossing is upon us. We must honor Rose for the journey that is before her. Taivyn, it is good she will have you here with her." The look in the Master's eyes told Taivyn what he needed to know. He could stay. "Come now, the appointed time is here."

Rose looked at Taivyn. Her eyes – it was her eyes that would forever tell the story of the Dragon and the Rose.

Chapter 48
The Appointed Time

*"When you work you are a flute through whose heart
the whispering of the hours turns to music...And what is
it to work with love? It is to weave the cloth with
threads drawn from your heart, even as if your beloved
were to wear that cloth...."*

- Kahlil Gibran, *The Prophet*

The Forest – 11,000 BCE (6 months after GG)

Resting softly on a nearby granite stone, the tiny amphibian cooed a soft melody. To most, he would appear to be singing to himself, but those with "ears to hear" and "eyes to see" would understand quite immediately that his song was not for himself alone. A croak overlaid with a soft strumming of strings of a harp only half described this exotic tune, for this very song he sung always commenced as a beckoning call to a companion that he rarely met. Longingly, but with total faith, he continued his song. He had been singing for a very long time now according to most records. He sang and sang as he had been doing for years, for the time it takes to prepare for an event like this cannot be thrown together overnight.

All waited with bated breath. A singular point in history was upon them. Those watching looked to the sky and saw the stars begin to align in such a way as was predicted. Then the constellations crossed. The universal principle of "as above, so below" was occurring and so what happened almost simultaneously was expected and yet completely new.

The frog's tune that he'd been singing now began to change. A tiny creature jumped and catapulted to what some might consider the finish line, but he did not move. Then suddenly their two songs became one and what commenced as a singular tune soon became a musical masterpiece. A symphony of sound, so exquisite and spellbinding that no one made a move. This companion had waited long for this single moment in time, and now it was here. The skies opened and a golden silver light poured forth, engulfing all who stood near to the center of the sound. All stood perfectly still and present for just a moment to receive and honor the blessing that resulted from the auspicious event that they witnessed. And then it was show time!

****

A black raven circled overhead. Yuri had just arrived, but he was too late! He quickly discerned the status of the situation – the Crossing of the Frog and the

Mushroom had begun. There was nothing that could be done now besides staying the course. His message would just have to wait until after Rose crossed the Rainbow Bridge of Light. Interrupting the Crossing now would surely take them down a road from which there was no return.

Chapter 49
A Cat's Consultation

"Karma is the eternal assertion of human freedom...Our thoughts, our words, and deeds are the threads of the net which we throw around ourselves."

- Swami Vivekananda

Maine – 2005

Jedda walked to Lou's house slowly. And she took her time doing it. Still shaken from the appearance of that crazed man, coupled with her wildly uncanny experience with Vyn, Jedda was a mix of emotions that ranged from fear to sadness to excitement. Her thoughts were going off in a thousand different directions, all while wondering how safe she was in the moment. She pushed ideas of dark figures with scary eyes out of her mind for now. She would have plenty of time to think of that when she discussed it with Lou.

As confounding as it was, she turned her attention back to Vyn. She had no understanding why she'd just seen someone that looked just like Taivyn from the Forest, a time that existed thousands of years ago. *It must have something to do with what occurred at the Tor of Avalantia.* There certainly hadn't seemed to be anything out of the ordinary with Vyn, though. Then again she didn't believe she looked out of the ordinary either. There would have been no way of telling from their brief interaction that she was severely abnormal in every way. And in all fairness she couldn't know that about him, either.

She walked along and cut through the park, stopping here and there to admire the trees. She loved how they looked on nights like this: a star-filled sky and the moon only a crescent that gave off the tiniest sliver of light that seemed to complement its twinkling companions in the sky. Her attention focused on the ground; she kicked a stone pebble here and there. As she drew nearer, she could make out Lou's house. Rats! The lights were off. That wasn't a good sign. She must be out. She wouldn't be asleep; it was still much too early, and Lou said she never got jet-lagged. Lou was an early riser as much as she was a night owl. In all honesty, Jedda wasn't sure when the woman slept.

She bounded up to the door. The place was dark. With no car in the driveway, Jedda was sure Lou had left. Where in the world would she have gone? She should be resting. Not good. *I need to talk to her.* Jedda noticed a shadow move in the window. Isis! She knocked on the door and called out at the same time,

"Isis? Is that you?"

"Yes, why of course it's me. Who else would it be, for heaven's sake? Do come in. Lou locked the door, but you know where she keeps the key. I'm sure everyone does," Isis commented in her typically sarcastic tone. Jedda let herself in.

"Isis! But why didn't you go with Lou? Don't you miss each other? Where' s Lou gone off to at this time?" Jedda looked at her watch. 8:30pm. Jedda's parents still wouldn't be home from their dinner. Not at least for another hour. She was in the clear for now.

"Lou's gone to speak with one of her colleagues. Some things have occurred that have left her a bit concerned. You know Lou. Always a worrywart, that one. She'd plan for a hurricane if it might happen three years from now. Anyway, hopefully she'll be back soon. She forgot to feed me."

Jedda laughed, "Isis, that's ridiculous. How could she have forgotten to feed you?"

"As I said she is quite perturbed about a little matter."

"And what matter is that?"

"Well…." Isis didn't want to mention the bird's visit. She'd let Lou handle that. "It's pertaining to her cousin."

"Her cousin? She never talks about a cousin…."

"Well, they haven't spoken in ages and she hadn't even heard anything of him in quite some time. Almost ten years. Until now."

"Oh my! Isis, I wonder if that's who showed up at my house this evening."

"Malin showed up at your house?" Isis asked alarmed. "How could he know about you? We have been so careful! Damn him to hell! That man just won't stop. He doesn't know how much harm he could cause."

"Isis, who is Malin? Why haven't I heard of him before?"

"Be happy you haven't. It's no pleasant conversation. No pleasant conversation indeed. Nothing about that man is particularly warm and fuzzy. You know what I mean?"

"Well, I can't just sit around here waiting. I need answers. I need to gain clarity. Isis, I need to talk to the trees."

"Really? What part of 'there may be a slightly deranged person looking for you' was not clear?"

"Don't worry. I'm not going far. And I'm not going for a walk out there," Jedda pointed to the front windows that had a view of the sidewalk.

"Oh thank goodness. For a second, I thought you meant to say you were leaving somewhere."

"I am. But that way." She pointed toward the woods in the back.

Really? Did this girl ever stop? Did anyone? Why couldn't everyone just stay put? If everyone just stuck together surely they'd figure a whole lot more out. Oh well. Free will. Who ever made that rule up clearly hadn't been thinking straight at the time. Free Will. Bah!

"Would you let Lou know where I've gone please? Tell her to join me in the Faery Glen when she comes back." Then she really looked at the cat. Isis felt the girl's anxiety. "Isis, I'm really scared right now. I feel safe when I'm there...."

"All right. I'll let Lou know. I'm sure she'll be thrilled."

The cat managed her best grin, but it was clearly forced. For all the cat's sardonic hints, however, she really did understand.

Chapter 50
Do You Wish to Enter?

"Do you seek the road to Fairyland?
I'll tell; it's easy, quite.
Wait till a yellow moon gets up o'er
purple seas by night,
And gilds a shining pathway that is
sparkling diamond bright
Then, if no evil power be nigh to
thwart you, out of spite,
And if you know the very words to cast a spell of might,
You get upon a thistledown, and if the breeze is right,
You sail away to Fairyland along this track of light."

-Ernest Thompson Seton

Maine – 2005

J edda wandered through the woods. It was dark and the sounds of the night were everywhere. Save the small flashlight Jedda carried to illuminate her way, there was no light in this place. She arrived at the Faery

Glen tired and out of breath. She knew she would feel safe here. For now, her home was off limits. She couldn't risk being there if that wicked man were to return. At least not until her parents were home. Based on the crazed look in the man's eyes, she wasn't sure if her parents would be able to protect her, anyway. No, this was the safest place for now.

On the edge of Evolet Woods, the Fairy Glen had been known by locals for centuries. It was unknown how the field had ended up with this name; however, anyone who came here could take one guess. Enchantment hung in the air within this space. When one stepped onto the field just beyond the soft border of large rocks a sacred sweetness was felt through and through. The field glowed in the moonlight, while a soft magical light filled one from within. In the center of the field lay a centuries-old labyrinth. Constructed of thousands of small, smooth river stones, the classical seven-circuit pathway lay halfway between the border of rocks and the other side of the woods.

Jedda's face had become damp with tiny beads of perspiration, which she noticed as she lifted her fingers to brush a few strands of hair out of her face. She moved to enter the inner part of the Fairy Glen.

****

The whole ten minutes Vyn and Jedda had spent talking to one another he'd had these strange electric flutters within his heart and soul. He didn't know what to make of it. Usually pretty good at ignoring his feelings, he had figured he'd have no trouble brushing it off. Only he couldn't brush it off. Not only that, but the moment she had stepped off the bus and onto the ground, the cute and cuddly protective feeling he'd been experiencing as he sat with her turned into a terror-stricken urge to shield and protect at all costs. Instead of lessening, it quickly became a raging boar that wouldn't let him rest. He had a bad feeling – a really bad feeling.

As he approached the stop where she alighted the bus, his brisk jog turned into a slow gait. Not wanting to be discovered for fear of alarming her, he proceeded with the utmost caution. He was sure this could be categorized as stalking. Of course he meant her no harm. Quite the opposite, he wanted to make sure that whatever he was feeling was completely in his head. He thought he might be going mad. What was he doing anyway? Following a young girl, at night no less! He must be out of his mind. Just as he had arrived at the stop where she'd gotten off he noticed her go inside a dark house. His brain told him he should be happy because she had made it safely home. He was about to end this ridiculous charade and just turn and go home. She had clearly made it home safely.

Then he saw someone leave out the front door. It was *her*! What was she doing? She slid around the side of the house and slipped into the woods out back. What the heck? Was she crazy? He'd hoped she wasn't out doing some strange ritual in the forest. Why did they always have to be at night? And who would do them alone? No thank you. He knew enough about stirring up the supernatural to know he didn't want to be playing with otherworldly spirits by himself at night.

Now he had to follow her. After all, it was his moral obligation to do so. She didn't need to know. He'd only make sure she was safe and that no harm came to her. Hopping from one tree to the next, he made sure to maintain his cover. If trees could talk…well, he knew they could; he just didn't speak their language. He wondered if she did….

A wolf howled in the distance, ripping the silence to shreds. The rustling of the leaves made the young boy's skin crawl. A presence of something hung low and to the ground like a snake –but nothing was there. Vyn started to back up, fearing that he was walking right into something…some darkness that hovered all around. This darkness was thicker than the dark of the night sky. It was dense, and made the air hard to breathe…*Meow*.

Vyn jumped two feet high. What in the name of mercy? A cat. A long black cat sat there staring at him. What was a cat doing out here? The cat stared long and hard. The feline finished his analysis of Vyncent and must have determined he wasn't a threat because he released his gaze and relaxed. The cat meowed one more time and rubbed against Vyn's legs. The boy reached down to pet him just as he meowed one last time before darting away. Vyn lost sight of him. He refocused. When he regained sight of Jedda, he noticed the cat by her side. At this point he was sure she was doing some strange ritual. She's probably some self-proclaimed witch just out for a nightly constitution and

a little ritual work he assured himself. No big deal.
Only that's weird.

****

Meow!
Jedda looked to her left to find Artemis sprawled
upon one of the large border rocks. His eyes were two
green flames that stared at her.

"Oh, Artemis! You blessed creature, you! You
followed me. But how did you…?" *How in the world
would he have gotten here?* Jedda had no idea how he'd
managed to follow her all this way; it was practically
impossible. She had taken a bus! She stared at her cat
with both adoration and disbelief.

"How did you know I'd be needing a friend? I have
to admit I really don't want to be alone right now. Will
you come with me toward the labyrinth nearer to the
other side of the woods?"

Jedda had felt a soft nudge within her heart to go in
that direction. She looked at her beloved cat. Artemis
did an adorable roll belly up, meowed, and climbed
down. She set off with her furry companion, moving
easily through the loosely strewn rock border. As they
neared the west side of the labyrinth, Jedda looked up
into the night sky. A movement among the firmament
disturbed the stillness. A shooting star. Simultaneously
a whirling movement on the edge of the forest just
beyond the labyrinth caught both of their attention.

Absent were any feelings of fear and foreboding.
Only the familiar sense of longing accompanied this

mysterious spinning light. Jedda did not even hesitate. The closer she got to the whirling light, the more it began to take on a form. The color shifted from a soft white glow to a pale shimmering blue, the color of the sea. Then where the light had been, a figure now stood in its place. The figure was shining as if born of the light itself. Robes of liquid silk in silver and milky white adorned its form.

"Welcome, Rose." The figure's voice was a gentle whistle that sounded like a flute being played on the seaside. The figure had little moving wisps of light fluttering around it. They blinked, dancing to the harmony of its words.

"Hello. I hope I have not intruded by coming here at this time." The tiny creatures floated over to Jedda when she spoke, surrounding her.

"Nonsense. There is only one time in divine time and that is NOW. The gateway has been opened. Do you wish to enter?"

The wisps started coming into focus. Jedda was beginning to see them more clearly. She could make out tiny forms within the light. Tiny little sea dragons and floating beings with little tails. Some had webbed feet or wings. They were beautiful. Never had she seen anything like them before.

"What are they?"

"They are called wisps. They work with the light. This particular group is getting ready to make its descent to the Earth plane. They are young beings that have not yet chosen the form to which they are best suited to work. They are watery beings by their nature.

They have taken a liking to you. If you choose to enter they shall assist you."

"I, well…I do *wish* to enter…I was going to wait for someone, though…."

"I know. You wait for the Keeper. However she will not be able to attend at the appointed time. I will ask again. Do you wish to enter?"

Jedda looked around. She saw the tiny creatures moving on the forest floor. They floated up either side of her. She felt their love and purity. Wisps.

"Yes. Yes, I wish to enter."

"Then the initiation is begun."

****

The last thing she noticed was a face in the distance. *Vyn…What is he doing here?* That was her last thought before…darkness. Vyn rushed to where Jedda had stood only moments before, but she was gone. Only darkness remained.

"I will find you," he whispered.

Chapter 51
The Crossing

"The Way is patterned on nature."

- Lao Tzu, Tao Te Ching

The Forest – 11,000 BCE (6 months after GG)

S he stood poised and ready, but not without a tiny trace of trepidation for what lay ahead. Feeling the weight of responsibility upon her shoulders of what was being asked of her, of what she'd most definitely agreed to, she was steadfast in her determination. And yet she naturally hesitated, for what lay waiting on the other side for her, she knew not.

The bridge expanded before her as far as the eye could see and beyond. Its structure gleamed before her eyes, braided strands of light in all the colors of the rainbow. Three steps rose up from the ground to a small platform where two large columns marked the entranceway to the bridge.

She glanced over her shoulder. Peering at the crowd gathered below, she allowed their support to be her strength as she took this step into the unknown. She needed reassurance now more than ever.

The multi-colored ropes of light sparkled in the twilight. The Rainbow Bridge of Light. What would it be like when she made it to the other side? She was aware that walking across the bridge would change everything forever. She breathed deeply of the sweet air and shimmering light composed of crystal atoms all around her. The bridge was verily a link between two worlds, that of Human and that of Faerie.

The faery girl felt sad. She studied the faces of those that stood behind her. She focused on each one. She came to rest her eyes on her mother: *I will miss her so…* she thought to herself. Then her eyes fell upon Taivyn – words could not express the depth of feeling that moved between these two souls.

Yuri landed on the edge of the right column. "Lady Rose, Good Day to you. I have come to see you off. However I have also come to bring you fair warning…."

"Warning? Is something wrong?" Rose felt apprehensive.

"It is just that you need to be aware of the risks of the journey ahead…."

"What risks?" Rose asked, her concern growing.

"As you begin to walk across the bridge, you will enter a kind of limbo state. Existing neither here nor there, you will become invisible to us for a time. During this time even I will not be able to reach you. You will be lost to us."

"Lost?" Rose did not like the sound of that. She had never been "lost" before.

"Yes. Until you reach the other side, that is."

Yuri waited for Rose to comprehend. "Lady Rose, no matter what happens, you must keep moving forward. There is no going back. Once you step onto the bridge, you have begun the journey. Do you understand?"

Rose felt the nervousness that came with this choice throughout the whole of her ethereal being. She didn't even know faeries could feel nervous until now. She was leaving behind her whole known existence. Somewhere just beyond that anxiousness she felt a calm resolve.

Rose nodded in understanding.

"I bid you a safe journey then." His squawk was like a seal that both blessed and marked the commencement.

Rose turned one last time to those who stood waiting. The tears made her eyes twinkle like a sunlit lake. She smiled. Then she returned her gaze to study the bridge. She used her heart intention to activate the bridge. The bridge flickered and flashed. The connection with the bridge had been made. She would not look back again. Moving beyond the two columns, she entered the bridge. She took several steps, and then Rose was gone.

Those standing in wait were so still they almost held their breath. They would stand in vigil for three days and wait for Rose to appear on the other end. With her soft, delicate hands, Elysinia held tightly the crystal. The Frog and the Mushroom would commune for three days. It was a song; it was a dance; it was a meeting of power. It was this energy that the crystal harnessed and directed. It had taken the efforts of several including Elysinia to focus this raw power. And focus it they had for the good of the whole, thus the Rainbow Bridge had been created.

No one saw the Dark One who lurked in the shadows, waiting for the right moment when he, too, might use the power of the Crossing of the Frog and the Mushroom. And so he waited and watched, keen observer, crystal of his own in hand.

Then the ground shook. Thunder sounded as if ripping the atoms in the atmosphere to shreds. A reddish pink lightning never before seen struck and shattered the sky. Chaos. Animals scrambled and dashed for cover. Screams were heard. Confusion. No one knew what was happening. And then everything went black.

Only darkness remained. For everyone.

The raven flew to and fro frantically. Dizziness. Vertigo. He had to find Elysinia and fast. He saw her below trying to regain control of the recording quartz. The Frog and the Mushroom were still in communion. They were the only thing unaffected by the jolt that had just shaken the Earth.

Yuri flew back and forth, and then circled. He noticed the Dark One perched next to a large boulder reveling in the shadows. What had he done? He saw the crystal in his hand – a yellow light that flickered and dimmed. Crystals detested being used for anything but pure intentions. The second recording must have diluted the event's power, causing the bridge to fall momentarily.

Yuri flew down to where Elysinia and the others were. Only the faery elders remained holding the energy. The others had been taken out by the blow. They would recover, but not in time to offer their efforts to sustain the bridge.

"Elysinia! The Dark One has found us and is recording the Crossing of the Frog and the Mushroom," Yuri said. The bird sounded faint.

"That must have split the energy," Elysinia yelled. Her voice was raised in an attempt to be heard among the chaos. "The bridge collapsed. It was only momentarily, but it did collapse." The bridge had returned; alas, there had been a break in its continuity.

"Do you think Rose is going to make it?" Yuri asked, still out of breath.

"Only time will tell."

Three days came and went. Maob stood by, pleased that his ploy had so far been successful. He let himself bask in the glory, imagining the fruition of the dark plan he'd been scheming for so long.

Many had remained to hold open the Bridge of Light. Everyone was exhausted. They could barely hold on, they had expended so much. Many of them wondered if it were all in vain, seeing as the Bridge had been broken. It was possible Rose would not emerge on the other side – ever.

They didn't want to let go until they were sure. And yet they would not be sure until they saw her. Finally their tired bodies and souls gave way. They couldn't manage that level of intensity any longer; one by one they began to drop. The faery elders were the last to go. Seamone and Leori tired first. Aolana held on as long as she could. Then she released and collapsed. Their forms were weakened and blinking in and out of the Earth Plane. A great toll it had taken on all of them. Elysinia held out the longest. At the end of the fourth day, there was still no sign of Rose. Elysinia could hold the light no longer. She fell to the ground and lost consciousness.

When she came to, Maob was gloating over her, like a sneaky worm with a crooked smile. The humans were standing around, too. Many had fallen unconscious at the original blast created as a result of Maob's meddling. All had recovered and were standing around waiting for Elysinia to regain consciousness. They noticed Maob, but did not care. He was the least of their concerns – or so they thought. Taivyn stepped forward and knelt down beside Master Ra-Ma'at. The Master hadn't left Elysinia's side since he had recovered himself.

"Master, what happened to Rose?"

Elysinia wept. She wept for humankind and for the teachings that might not survive the Age of Sleep. Most of all, she wept for her daughter. Rose was lost. And there was nothing she, nor anyone else, could do.

A sense of loss suddenly overcame Taivyn. "Not again! I can't lose you again!"

There had to be something he could do. Something….

"I will find you," he whispered.

Epilogue

"When the man in the fiery red garment of the sun appears to our grandfathers and grandmothers, the last part of the Great Change of life on earth will begin."

-Hopi Prophecy

It Comes...

The darkness swept over the land like a shadow that swallows its prey. It rolled and thundered, and yet it did not overstep its bounds. For even the darkness knows its place. And those who work with it would do well to know it, too. Like anything in life, the darkness has a place. It would have 13,000 years to roar and rumble about – making a statement, as it had not been seen or heard in quite some time. But the time was now. And it was coming. Like a bubbling cauldron of compressed hot energy it gurgled and fizzed. It spit and spat until it was ready to come forth. And now it was nearly ready.

Made in the USA
Middletown, DE
25 October 2020

22744979R00201